Protecting Jessyka

Protecting Jessyka

SEAL of Protection
Book 6

By Susan Stoker

Table of Contents

Note from the Author

After the first few SEAL of Protection books came out, I started to get questions from readers if "Jess," from *Aces Bar and Grill*, was going to get a story. I always smiled, proud that the little teasers of Jessyka I'd put in the other books had done their job… made readers interested in her story.

I wanted to have a heroine who was disabled, but it didn't faze her. She didn't talk about it, it didn't slow her down… it was just a part of who she was and a normal part of her life.

I've seen comments from readers who complained that each story in the series was the "same". I've tried really hard to make them different, but I *am* a fan of the damsel in distress… and while most of my heroines are tough women in their own right, they all need a hand in the end.

With that in mind, I tried to make Jess's story a *bit* different. I hope you'll see what I mean when you read it.

Thank you all for your support of the SEALs. From the messages I've received online, to the support from readers at book signings, to the day in and day out encouragement from my PA, Amy—thank you.

As long as you, the reader, keeps on enjoying my stories, I'll keep writing them. Enjoy Jessyka and Benny's story.

Chapter One

BENNY PUSHED AWAY the plate of microwaved food sitting in front of him at his little table in his kitchen. He loved to cook, was quite good at it even, but he had no desire to whip up a grand meal for one.

Ever since his SEAL teammates, and friends, had found the loves of their lives, they'd spent less and less time together. It wasn't as if Benny begrudged his friends finding a woman to love and protect. He loved Ice, Alabama, Fiona, Summer, and Cheyenne as if they were his own sisters. He'd fight and die for them, simply because they loved his friends. But now he could see what was missing in his own life.

Benny had seriously considered asking for a transfer to another SEAL team. He knew it would rip his guts out to do it, but he didn't know how much longer he could go seeing what his friends had, and knowing it was out of his own reach.

He took a long drink from the glass of water he'd poured to go with his crappy dinner and thought back to the last time they'd all gotten together at *Aces Bar and Grill*. It was a small bar, but was always clean and was relatively peaceful. It was, admittedly, a pick up bar, that's how they found it in the first place. But since they'd been eating and drinking there for a while, it now felt more like home.

Benny knew he and his friends turned heads wherever they went. They used to go to the bar to hook up with women, but as each team member found the woman meant just for them, their reason for meeting up there changed. Now they enjoyed the atmosphere and the camaraderie they shared. But they were SEAL members. They were muscular men, who women seemed to find attractive.

Benny was the youngest on the team. He was six feet tall with short brown hair. Women in the past had told him he had unique eyes, the color of molten chocolate. Benny didn't know about that, he'd always thought they were just plain brown.

Over the time Benny and his teammates had been going to *Aces*, they'd gotten to know the names of the servers and bartenders, and everyone in return, knew who their team was as well. Unfortunately, it was also the place where Cheyenne, Summer, and Alabama had been snatched right out from under Mozart's nose while the girls were there for a night out. Luckily it ended all right and no one was seriously hurt or killed.

Last week the entire team had gotten together for dinner, drinks, and conversation to try to push out the bad memories of what had happened there. Benny knew if it had been up to his friends, they never would've stepped foot in the place again, but the ladies, being the strong stubborn women they were, had insisted. They'd laughed, and the women had even shed a tear or two, but in the end, it had been the right decision to go back.

But something was bothering Benny about their visit. He couldn't get the look on Jess's face out of his head. Their usual waitress had limped up to their table, with the little lopsided gait she had, and when he had gently taken hold of her arm to keep her from leaving right away, she'd grimaced.

Every man around the table had taken notice, and hadn't liked it. It didn't take a genius to see it had hurt when Benny had taken hold of her arm, and he hadn't grabbed her, hadn't squeezed, had just stopped her from leaving. Now that Benny thought about it, Jess hadn't been acting the same. When they'd first met her she'd been bubbly and easy-going, always laughing and joking with all of them.

But last week, she'd been quiet and kept her eyes downcast. The long-sleeved shirts were new too. In fact, the more Benny thought about her, the more worried he got. Whoever was abusing her was smart. He was keeping his hands off her face, where the abuse would be the most obvious. If Jess had come in with a black eye or a split lip, none of the guys would have hesitated to say something.

But if he was leaving bruises or hitting her on her body where her clothes hid the marks, no one could be certain. Benny didn't like the thought of Jess being hurt though. He knew that for sure.

He hadn't really thought about Jess in *that* way... until now. She'd just always been there. She was a part of the bar experience. She was a good waitress, always refilling their drinks, always laughing with them, but giving them room when they needed it.

When the girls had been kidnapped from the bar, Benny knew Jess had immediately huddled with Fiona and Caroline to keep them calm. She'd taken them into a back office and stayed with them until the team thought it was safe for them to leave.

Thinking back, Benny suddenly felt bad. They'd taken advantage of her hospitality and nurturing nature. They'd taken their women away, but left Jess there without a thought to *her* safety.

Benny just couldn't reconcile how good Jess had been with the team's women and how caring she was, with someone who'd stay with a man who abused her. There had to be a reason, but Benny couldn't think of what it might be.

He pushed up from his kitchen table, suddenly on a

mission. He couldn't go another moment without checking on Jess. He had a bad feeling in his gut, and a SEAL never dismissed those feelings.

Jess was probably fine. She was most likely at the bar and she'd call out a greeting, just as she always did, when he walked in.

Mind set, Benny grabbed his keys from the basket by the door and was headed to his car before he'd really made a conscious decision to move.

As his forgotten microwave dinner sat congealing on the counter, Benny pulled out of the parking lot of his apartment complex.

I'll just go and grab a burger, it's not like I'm really checking on her. I'm hungry. If she's there, great, I'll assuage my curiosity and then come back home. I'm sure she's fine. I'm just overreacting.

Chapter Two

JESSYKA ALLEN SIGHED. Her week had sucked. Actually the last month had sucked. She sighed again. Shit. Her *life* sucked. She had no idea how she'd gotten to where she was… stuck, with not many options open to her. She never thought she'd be the type of person who'd stay with someone who hurt her, but here she was.

It was always so easy to say, "The first time someone hit me, I'd be gone," but in real life it turned out it was much easier to say than to do.

Jess had grown up in a suburb of Los Angeles. Her parents weren't rich, but they weren't poor either. She was able to get the clothes she wanted and she had good friends in high school. She wasn't the most popular girl in school, but she also wasn't an outcast either.

Jessyka had been born prematurely, and as a result, one leg was shorter than the other. She didn't have any big dramatic story to tell about it, but it meant she limped, she'd always limped. She was teased growing up about it, but Jess had learned to mostly ignore people when they were rude.

There were times when her legs hurt, mostly because she had to overuse the muscles on her right leg to compensate for the shorter length of her left. Her parents had wanted her to try shoes with a lift on them, but Jess had hated them. They were mostly ugly and it was obvious the left shoe had a much larger sole on it than the right. So she limped.

She met Brian her junior year and they'd been friends throughout high school. It wasn't until they had graduated and taken classes at the local community college together that they'd started dating. Brian was fun and Jess had enjoyed spending time with him. After dating for a few years, it was obvious they weren't going to ever get married or have a future together. Brian had a temper, and Jess was completely laid back. She refused to fight back with him when he did turn on her, and that usually made him even angrier.

After they'd stopped being boyfriend and girlfriend, their relationship improved. Brian seemed to settle down and didn't seem as angry.

When Jess's parents moved across the country and she needed a place to live, Brian offered to let her move into the extra bedroom in his townhouse. Jess agreed on the spot. It had seemed to be the perfect arrangement.

It seemed even better when Jess met Tabitha. Tabitha was Brian's niece. His sister lived in a townhouse in the same complex as they did. Tabitha was ten when they'd met and Jess loved her on sight. She was a chubby kid, but had the biggest heart. Brian's sister, Tammy, was a mess though. She was a single mother and worked all the time. When she wasn't working, she still wasn't around much, so Jess became like Tabitha's second mother.

Tabitha was an unusually sensitive child though. She took everything to heart. Jess had seen Tabitha cry her eyes out when she'd seen a dead feral cat on the road next to the apartment complex one day. Jess had tried to console her, but Tabitha stayed in a funk for at least a week after that.

Brian didn't have any patience for his niece. He told Jess she was a baby and a whiner and would never get anywhere in the world.

Over the last four years, Brian had turned his harsh words onto Tabitha too. He didn't care who he put her down in front of, and he started haranguing Jessyka as well. It had gotten to a point where Jess knew Tabitha was depressed. She'd tried to talk to Tammy about it, but Tammy had blown her off and told her to mind her own business.

In the last couple of months, Brian had started to lash out at Jess again. It had started with words, but had quickly escalated to shoving, pushing, and, finally, hitting. Jess never knew what would set him off. He was completely unstable. One minute he'd be laughing and the next he'd be in her face screaming at her, telling her what a crippled loser she was.

Jess knew she had to get out, but she'd gotten complacent. Being a waitress didn't bring in that much money, and she knew she didn't have enough to move out on her own just yet. She could probably fly to Florida and live with her parents for a while, but she didn't want to leave Tabitha. The girl was fourteen and something wasn't right.

Jessyka worried about her all the time. Tabitha was withdrawn and sad. Jess spent as much time as she could with her and tried to cheer her up. It was hard though, because after the last time Jess had tried to talk with Tammy about her daughter, Tammy had told Tabitha Jess wasn't welcome in their apartment anymore.

So now Tabitha had to either come over to her apartment, and risk having Brian be there and messing with her head, or they'd have to go out. If they went out, Jess had to spend money on lunch, ice cream, or whatever. Money she should be saving to get her own place. It was a vicious circle, but Jess knew she couldn't abandon Tabitha. She loved her and Tabitha needed her. So she stayed.

Jess figured she could take it. It wasn't as if Brian was *really* hurting her. She could take the bruises. It was no big deal.

But deep down, she knew it *was* a big deal. Jess worked in a bar. She'd seen it time and time again with the patrons. She'd seen how the violence escalated. Jess felt stuck. She wanted to go, but knew leaving would mean bad things for Tabitha. She just didn't know what to do anymore. It felt like she had the world on her shoulders.

Jess rolled her head to try to release some tension and winced. Damn. She'd forgotten about her shoulder. Brian had wrenched it that afternoon before she'd left to go to work. Jess had been visiting Tabitha and had come back into the apartment with just enough time to change before having to leave for work.

"Where have you been?" Brian had inquired nastily.

"Visiting with Tabitha." Jess kept her voice flat, knowing if she threw any attitude, Brian would make her pay for it.

"I don't know why you bother. She's fat. She'll always be fat. She's stupid too. Tammy tells me all the time what a moron she is and how embarrassed she is by her."

"She's not stupid, Brian. I've read some of the stories she's written. She's actually very talented and I know she's going to be a famous author someday."

"What the hell do you know, crip? You're just as stupid as she is. Working as a damn waitress in a fucking bar. What a loser. You know everyone just makes fun of you behind your back don't you? I've seen them. You limp around the bar and everyone just laughs and bets on if you'll drop a tray or not."

Jess stared at Brian, not believing the words that were coming out of his mouth. How had they gotten to this point? What had she done for him to have such horrible feelings about her? They used to be friends.

Misunderstanding her look, Brian continued. "Surprised, crip? Yeah, they all laugh at you, especially the military guys. I bet you have fantasies about them doing you? Well, give it up. They only like the beautiful, perfect ladies."

Brian's words struck her hard, just as he'd meant them to.

"What's happened to us, Brian?" Jess couldn't help the words, she'd been thinking them and with his harsh words, they just popped out. "We used to be friends."

"Friends don't sponge off one another," he immediately returned. "I've been working my ass off for that construction company, and you bring home pennies and pretend you're putting in your fair share. Jesus, Jess, I can't believe you haven't already figured this out."

"But, Brian…" Jessyka started, not surprised when he interrupted her.

"No, Jess, you're pathetic." He came toward her and Jess took a step back.

"You limp around all day, you dress in drab shit clothes, and you expect everyone to love you." Brian grabbed her upper arm and squeezed, trying to make his point.

"I work my ass off and you coddle my niece. My sister hates you, you just don't see it. Fuck, I don't know why I put up with you."

Without warning, Brian lifted the hand that wasn't holding her and put it around her neck. He backed them up until she hit the wall behind them.

Jess drew in a quick breath and brought both hands up to grasp Brian's wrist.

"Brian, please…"

He squeezed her throat. "No, I'm done with this shit. You have until the end of the month and I want you out. Seriously. You have nine fucking days."

Jess just looked up at Brian. It didn't even look like the Brian she knew. His face was contorted with an irrational anger she'd never seen before. She opened her mouth to speak, to tell him whatever he needed to hear to placate him, but he tightened his grip on her neck.

Shit. He wasn't letting go. Jess's hands clawed at Brian's hand around her throat and wiggled, trying to make him lose his grip.

Finally, with a smirk, he let go. Before Jess could catch her breath and get away from him, he'd wrenched the arm he still had in his grasp, spun her around, and held it up against her back.

"I'm serious, crip. Nine days. Got it?"

Jess could only nod frantically and try to block out the pain of Brian wrenching her arm at an unnatural angle. She swallowed painfully, and prayed he'd let go of her.

When he did, Jess didn't even look back, just fled up the stairs to her room. She'd slammed the door and locked it behind her. Not that the flimsy lock would keep Brian out if he really wanted in, but it made her feel marginally better.

Now Jess was at work. She had to figure out what she was going to do. She didn't want to go back to the townhouse, even for the nine days Brian had given her, but she had nowhere else to go. None. She also didn't want to leave Tabitha. Somehow she knew the girl was only hanging in there because of her. Jess knew if she said it out loud to anyone, it'd sound conceited, but she knew, deep down inside, if Tabitha thought Jess had abandoned her, she'd break.

Jess picked up the heavy tray and tried not to wince. She had no idea what she was going to do, but she had to get through her shift first. Then she'd think about it.

BENNY PULLED INTO the parking lot of *Aces* and turned off his engine. He had no idea what he was really doing, but something in the back of his mind wouldn't let him let this go. Something was wrong, and he liked Jess. He didn't really know her, but he liked her nonetheless.

He pocketed his keys as he walked to the front door of the bar. Entering, it took a moment for Benny's eyes to adjust to the darkness. It was later than he'd been there in a long time. Usually the team and their women came around dinner time and ended up leaving around ten or so. At eleven, the bar was busy and the lights had been dimmed.

Benny looked around and didn't see Jess. He made his way to the bar and sat on a stool on the end so he could see the entire room. He ordered a draft beer and took his time nursing it. Ignoring the looks the two women across the room were giving him, he wasn't there to pick up a woman, he kept his eyes peeled for Jess.

Finally he saw her. Jess was his age, probably late twenties or early thirties. She had pale skin, which somehow made her look more fragile than she was. She was shorter than his six feet by a few inches. She was curvy, and as Benny noticed for the first time tonight, she filled out her clothes in a way which was sexy as hell.

She was struggling to hold on to a tray filled with empty bottles and glasses and make her way across the crowded bar. Benny stood up and went toward her.

It looked to Benny that Jess was limping more than

usual. He had no idea why she limped, he only knew that she always had. They'd all noticed it the first time they'd met her at the bar, and when Wolf had commented on it, she'd given him a death stare. No one had asked about it again. She was entitled to her secrets, and besides, it was kinda rude for Wolf to have asked in the first place.

He reached Jess just as she got bumped by someone behind her. She would've gone flying, but Benny grabbed the tray with one hand and her waist with the other. He spun them in a move that would've gotten them high points if it was being scored, and saved her, and the tray, from sprawling on the floor.

"Thanks," Jess breathed, thankful she wasn't sitting in the middle of the grimy floor surrounded by broken glass.

"You're welcome."

The voice was low and strangely familiar.

Jess looked up. Wow, it was one of the SEALs. She wasn't sure of his name. She'd heard all of their names more than once, but it was confusing as hell because sometimes she heard their nicknames and other times their real names. She couldn't keep them all straight.

The man continued to hold her to him, finally she shifted, trying to break his hold. He held on for another beat then finally let her go, brushing his hand along her hip in the process.

Jess held back a shiver. "I'll take that." She gestured toward the tray he was holding up. Some of the bottles had fallen over, but nothing was broken.

"Lead the way, Jess, I've got it."

Jessyka stared at him for a beat. "You know my name?"

"Yeah, I've only been eating here with my friends for an eon now and you're always our server. I know your name."

Jess blushed. Shit. Of course he knew who she was. She shook her head and tried to play it off. "Just checking. Come on." She turned her back on him and led him back to the busy bar. When they got there he finally allowed her to take the tray out of his hands and she placed it on the bar.

Turning back she said, "Thanks again, that would've sucked to have spilled all those bottles." Looking around she asked, "Where are your friends?"

Jess knew this guy was always here with the other SEALs. She'd watched them with a bit of jealously over the last few months. Most of the men were now either married or in a serious relationship. Jessyka had watched how they treated their woman. It was a mixture of tolerance and protectiveness with a bit of caveman thrown in. But it wasn't over-the-top. It looked delicious. If Jessyka had a man who looked at her like those men looked at their women, she didn't think she'd ever give him up.

"Don't know."

"What?"

The man smiled at her as if he knew she had slipped into a daydream for a moment. "I said, I don't know where my friends are. They're probably all at home with their women."

"Then why are you here?" Jess paused, then blushed. "Oh, never mind. Sorry. Yeah, why does any single man come to the bar? I'll just..." Her embarrassed words were cut short.

"I'm not here to pick up a woman, Jess. I'm here to check on you."

"Me?" Jess just looked at him incredulously.

"Yeah, you. I'm worried about you."

"Uh, I don't mean to be rude, but you don't even know me."

"Jess, remember what I said earlier in this conversation. I've been coming here for a while now. I know your personality has changed over the last few months. I know while you always limp, it's gotten worse. I know that the last time I saw you, I touched your arm and you flinched. I know you used to wear cute little tank tops and short sleeves, now you're wearing a damn turtleneck. This is Southern California and I can't remember the last time I've even seen someone wearing a fucking turtleneck. I'm a Navy SEAL, gorgeous, I've been trained to be observant. Maybe someone else wouldn't notice, but I have. I don't like it when women grimace when I touch them. I don't like knowing *why* they might do that. So I'm here because I'm worried about you."

Jess just stared at the handsome man standing next to her, baffled. As usual, her mouth opened before her brain could stop it. "I don't even know your name."

He smiled and shook his head. "Will you ever stop surprising me?" It was obviously a rhetorical question, because he continued without letting her answer. "I'm Kason. Kason Sawyer."

"Is that your real name or nickname?"

"Real name."

After a beat, Jess asked, "Are you going to tell me your nickname? I know you all have them."

"No. I don't like it, but I earned it fair and square. The guys call me by my nickname, but you won't."

"But…"

"Are you all right?"

"Kason…"

"Don't lie to me, Jess."

"Jessyka!"

She turned to see the bartender gesturing at her then to the drinks he'd lined up at the waitress station.

"I gotta go."

"When do you get off tonight?"

Jess stared at Kason for a moment. It wasn't that she didn't trust him. Hell, if she couldn't trust a Navy SEAL, she couldn't trust anyone. She was just still confused about why he was there. Jess didn't actually believe it was because he was worried about her. Yeah, he probably did notice all those things about her, but he didn't know her. So he couldn't *really* be worried about her.

"Two."

"I'll wait."

"Kason…"

"I said, I'll wait."

Jess looked at him for a beat, then turned abruptly and headed for the drinks she had to deliver. She didn't have time to worry about Kason. He'd get tired of whatever game he was playing and bolt. She had more important things to worry about. Namely, where the hell she was going to live and how she was going to come up with enough money to find a place of her own in nine days.

Chapter Three

BENNY WATCHED AS Jess worked the rest of her shift. Focusing one hundred percent of his attention on her, he could see she was definitely not the same person as he'd met when they first started coming to the bar. Oh, she was still efficient and good at what she did, but she was different.

She used to touch people all the time. She'd lay a hand on their arm, or she'd touch their hand briefly when they handed her money. She used to laugh more and flirt more. She didn't smile as much and she didn't flirt at all.

She was completely focused on the job at hand... getting drinks to patrons and collecting money. The more Benny thought about it, the more he was bothered by her clothes as well. All waitresses knew in order to increase tips, it was good to wear clothes that showed a little skin. Benny couldn't see any skin on Jess except for her face and hands.

Benny knew Jess was uncomfortable with him being

there, but he didn't let it stop him. He joked with the bartender and rebuffed every woman who approached him. He was here for Jess, nothing else. He wasn't even tempted by any of the ladies that came on to him. In the past, he probably would've jumped at the chance to spend a sexually charged night with any of the women that were there, but not tonight. He was completely focused on Jess.

Benny watched as two o'clock came and Jess cashed out. She shoved her tips into the front pocket of her jeans and disappeared down the hall where the office was. She came back a moment later with her purse over her shoulder and headed for the door, without looking around for him.

Benny quickly followed her and gave a chin lift to the bouncer. "I've got it. I'll make sure she's safe."

The bouncer nodded, he knew Benny, had seen him around and knew he was a SEAL.

Benny came up next to Jess as she walked into the parking lot. "Can I take you home?"

Jess stopped in the middle of the lot and turned to Kason. "Why are you following me?"

"We've already been over this, but I can rehash it if you need me to."

Jess shook her head impatiently, at the end of her rope. "Look, Kason, I've had a bad week. Hell, a bad month, and I don't need you fucking with me. I've seen your friends. I'm too young for all of you. I don't do one-night stands. I'm not looking for a military guy. I'm broke, crippled, and too tired to deal with whatever it is you want out of me tonight. So just back off and let me go. Okay?"

As if he didn't hear a word she said, Kason simply said, "Let me take you home."

Jess sighed and looked down at the ground. She looked back at the bar then turned to Kason. "I usually take the bus."

"Please."

"Fuck. All right, Kason. You can take me home."

Benny took Jess's elbow in his and steered her the other way to his car. He clicked the locks as they were walking up and opened the door for her. He waited until she was seated before closing the door and walking around to the other side. Still without a word, he started the engine and pulled out of the lot.

"Where to?"

Jess startled. Duh, of course he didn't know where she lived. "I live in the Pinehurst townhouses over on Sunshine Way. Do you know them?" Jess watched as he nodded.

"Put your head back and close your eyes, gorgeous. Relax. I got this."

Jess blew out a half laugh and did as Kason said. It wasn't because he ordered it, it was because she was exhausted. She hurt. She was tired. She was stressed. The small break to let down her guard was unexpected, but appreciated.

Jess felt the car slow after a while, then stop. She opened her eyes and started in surprise. They weren't at her place.

"Where the hell are we?" She demanded.

Benny turned in his seat so he was facing Jess. He'd driven to a local park that he knew wasn't too seedy, and parked the car. He was going to talk to her whether she wanted to or not.

"I know we don't really know each other, but you need a friend, Jess, and I'm it. I'm not fucking with you. You aren't too young for me. Hell, we're probably only like five years apart in age. I'm not looking for a one-night stand with you, I don't give a damn how much money you have and you aren't fucking crippled. If I hear you say that about yourself one more time, I'm gonna take you over my knee. And you'll never be too tired to let me be a sympathetic ear for you. That's what I want. Now talk."

Jess just looked at Kason for a beat, thinking back to what she'd said to him in the parking lot of the bar. "Did you really just address every single thing I said earlier? How did you remember all of it?"

"Jess, focus."

"I *am* focused, Kason!" Jess exclaimed. "Seriously!

That was impressive."

"Did you hear what I said?"

Jess nodded and rubbed her temples. "Yeah. I'm sorry. I was being honest when I said I'd had a bad day. I'm sorry for being a bitch."

"You aren't a bitch."

"I can be."

"I have no doubt." Jess watched as Kason chuckled. "All of my friend's women can be. It's not a big deal. But I meant what I said earlier tonight. I'm worried about you. Talk to me. Please?"

"I don't know what you want me to say. I feel awkward." Jess picked at a thread hanging off the bottom of her shirt. "I'm not in the habit of spilling all my problems to people I don't know."

"I'm Kason. I'm a Navy SEAL. I've been in the Navy for about ten years. I love my friends. I'd give my life for any one of them and the same goes for their women. I love to cook and I'm good at it. I can pick a lock faster than anyone else on my team. I hate my nickname, but the guys won't change it. It's an inside joke between us now. Hell, if they *did* let me change it, I probably wouldn't. My favorite color is brown. I'd love to own a piece of land someday where I could go days without seeing anyone. Most of the time I don't like people, they're rude and conceited and self-absorbed. I've seen more shit in my lifetime than any person has a right to.

I love dogs and hope to have at least four when I get my piece of land somewhere. I'll always be a bit rough around the edges, but if I ever find a woman who can put up with me, I'll put her first in all things in my life. I've seen how my teammates are with their women and I want what they have. I'm the odd man out on my SEAL team right now and I hate it. I've been thinking about transferring, but haven't told any of them yet."

He stopped talking and Jess just stared at him. Finally she whispered, "Why did you tell me all that?"

"I want to get to know you, Jess. I'm spilling my guts to you in the hopes it'll make you feel less awkward and so you'll talk to me about what the hell is going on with you."

Jess licked her lips and picked at her thumbnail. She thought about what Kason had said. He really had shared some pretty personal stuff with her.

"Jess," Benny said taking hold of one of her hands so she had to stop picking at her fingernail. "Look at me."

When she did, Benny continued. "I consider us friends. We've known each other for a while now. We might not be the type of friends to go and get a manicure together and spend all day shopping, but I've seen you around enough to know when something is different. Let me help. Or at least let it out. It'll help. I promise."

Jess sighed. She loved the feel of her hand in his, but

knew she couldn't get used to it. She decided to copy him, but start with the easy stuff first.

"My name is Jessyka... spelled y-k-a, not i-c-a. I think my parents were drunk when they filled out the birth certificate." She smiled so he'd know she was kidding. "I grew up around LA and my parents are now living the high life in Florida. I like the color pink and I love dogs, especially hounds. I want a basset hound, a bloodhound, and a coonhound when I can get a place of my own. I'm currently a waitress and I make crap money at it, but interestingly enough, I like it. I meet lots of neat people." She smiled at Kason, but stopped talking. Now for the hard stuff.

"It's my roommate."

Benny sighed in relief. Thank God, she was talking to him about what was really bothering her. He loved hearing more about Jess and her life, but he wanted to know more about what was going on with her. Hopefully he'd have time to get more into the easy stuff later. "What about her?"

"Not her, him."

Benny tensed. A guy? She was living with a guy? He knew there was a guy involved somehow, but she was living with him? Fuck. "Go on. What about him?"

"Long story short, we met in high school, started dating while we were taking classes. After we graduated, we stopped dating, but were friends. I moved in with him because I needed a place to stay and he didn't seem to care. We're... having issues now."

"Why the hell would he want to stop dating you?"

"Huh?" Jess couldn't figure out how Kason's mind worked. He never said what she was expecting him to.

"Why weren't you dating? What the hell is wrong with him?"

"Nothing, I guess. We just didn't have a spark anymore."

"Moron."

Jess wasn't sure she heard Kason's mumbled word right, but she continued on without asking him to repeat it. "So anyway, we're having issues and I need to move out. But I'm worried about his niece. She's... vulnerable, and I'm afraid if I move out she'll do something rash."

"Does she live there too?"

"No, but she lives in the same complex and I see her all the time. She spends all her time, when she isn't at school and I'm not at work, with me."

Kason squeezed her hand. "I know you're leaving some important chunks out here, gorgeous, because I'm not seeing the problem so far." He brought his other hand over and ran his index fingers over the material of her shirt at her throat. "But I'm guessing part of it is whatever you're hiding under this."

Jess jerked back away from his touch, afraid he'd

pull down her turtleneck.

"Easy, Jess," Benny murmured, drawing back and giving her some space.

"It's…"

"Don't tell me it's nothing," Kason growled out, not sounding like the easy going man she'd been talking to for the last fifteen minutes. Jess thought it was almost scary how he could change so quickly.

"And don't flinch away from me. Fuck." He put both hands on the steering wheel and leaned his forehead against his hands for a moment before turning his head, leaving his head resting on his hands, and looked at her.

"We were on a mission once. I can't tell you where and I can't tell you why, but suffice to say it was in a country that didn't have the kind of women's rights we have here in the United States. I've never been so disgusted in all my life watching the women over there get beaten, kicked, and berated openly. No one cared. No one stood up for them. Kids were married off at age twelve to men four times their age. You never, *ever* have to worry about me physically hurting you. I know you probably don't believe me, but dammit, Jess. Try."

Jessyka took a deep breath. "I know it Kason. I do. It's just…"

"I know what it's just," Kason reassured her. "What can I do to help you?"

"What do you mean?"

"I mean, I'm your friend. What can I do to help you? Do you need help moving? Do you want me to get the girls to meet with your friend so she has some other good role models to look up to? Do you need money? Want me to beat up your roommate? Tell me what you need."

"You want to help me?"

"Jesus, Jess," Benny teased. "Pay attention! Yes, I want to help you."

"I-I don't know."

"Okay, well, why don't we start with exchanging phone numbers? That way when you figure it out, you can let me know." Benny didn't push, even though he wanted to.

"Uh, okay. Yeah. I'd like that." The more Jess thought about it, the more she *did* like it. She needed time to think about Kason and his offer of friendship and help.

They exchanged numbers and there was silence in the cab as they punched in each other's contact information. Jess startled when her phone vibrated with a new text. She smiled seeing it was from Kason, and looked up at him.

"Figured I'd make sure you didn't give me a pizza delivery boy's number."

Jess just shook her head and looked down at the text

he'd sent.

I'm always just a text away.

She looked up at Kason, not knowing what to say.

"I know we didn't really solve anything, but I hope you know I'm one hundred percent serious when I say I want to be your friend, Jess. You aren't alone and if you need anything, just call me. I'll be pissed if you don't. I sure as hell don't want you going back to your place with that fucker there, but you don't know me well enough yet to let me put you up somewhere. Use my number if you need it. Please."

"I have no idea why you want to be my friend, but thank you. It's been a long time since I've felt like I've had one."

Having the urge, and not resisting, Benny reached out a hand and slowly caressed Jessyka's face. Then he slid his hand around until it was resting on the back of her neck and he drew her gently and awkwardly in the small space of the car toward him. He leaned over and kissed her forehead and then rested his head against hers.

"Trust me, Jess."

Benny felt her nod slightly. He leaned back, squeezed her neck reassuredly, then let go.

"How about we get you home? It's late, you're tired, and I've got to get up in about an hour and a half for

PT."

"Okay."

When Benny pulled up to the townhouse Jess said she lived in, he put the car in park and said, "Stay."

He then walked around the car and opened the door for her. Jess just shook her head and climbed out. Kason walked her all the way to the front door, even though she'd insisted she was fine. He leaned in and once again kissed her on the forehead. "I'll see you later. Be safe."

Jess nodded and when Kason pulled back said, "Thank you."

"You're welcome. Don't be a stranger. I expect you to text."

"Okay."

"Okay."

"Bye, gorgeous."

"Bye, Kason."

Jessyka opened the door and cautiously entered the townhouse. The last thing she wanted was for Brian to be there waiting up for her. He wasn't. The place was quiet. Jess quickly headed up the stairs to her room and sighed in relief when she was in her room with the door locked.

She hated being scared of Brian, but she could still feel his fingers wrapped around her neck. He'd been pissed, and she hadn't even done anything. She knew nine days was too long. She had to do something sooner than that.

The phone Jess had been clutching in her hand vibrated. She looked down and smiled.

Sleep well. Talk to you later.

She didn't know how the hell she'd gotten lucky enough to have Kason decide he wanted to be her friend, but she certainly wasn't going to complain. It seemed like the only good thing that had happened to her in the last year.

Nite. ltr.

She expected that to be the end of it, but her phone vibrated again soon after she'd hit send.

You're one of those people who write in text speak aren't you?

Jess couldn't help the small laugh that escaped her mouth. She couldn't remember the last time she'd laughed out loud.

Appntly so. Don't txt & drve
I'm at a stop light. Good night, gorgeous.
Gd nite

Jess turned off her phone with a smile. Maybe tomorrow, well today, would be a better day. It certainly started out all right.

Chapter Four

BENNY COULDN'T STOP thinking about Jessyka. It'd been days since he'd seen or talked to her, with the exception of the few texts they'd exchanged. They had all been initiated by him, but she'd always responded, which made Benny feel a little bit better.

He hadn't had a chance to get back to the bar, but he also didn't want to seem like a stalker. Benny trusted Jess would get a hold of him if she needed to. He couldn't force her.

The bottom line was that Benny liked her. He couldn't say he really knew her all that well, but he hadn't lied when he'd told her that he liked what he'd seen so far.

Benny had a conversation with Dude about Jess the night before. He'd gone to his house to have dinner with him and Cheyenne. It seemed like the guys were "passing him around" like a lost puppy. Each week someone new would ask if he wanted to come over for dinner. Benny never refused, first because he liked his friends and their women, and second because it kinda sucked sitting at home alone.

Benny supposed he could go out and find a woman to bring home for the night, but he didn't really have the urge, especially since his little chat with Jessyka.

After dinner and a movie, Cheyenne had gone up to bed, and Dude had asked Benny how he was doing. Benny took the chance to bring up Jess.

"Remember the waitress at the bar the night we all went out last?"

"Yeah, Jess, right?"

"Yeah. We all saw the shape she was in that night. I couldn't get her out of my mind. I mean, I feel like I know her, with how much time we spend in that damn place. I think we've only been served by someone different a few times."

Dude had nodded. "Yeah, she looked a bit rough. Didn't like the way she flinched when you touched her."

"Yeah, me either. I went to the bar the other night and she looked even worse."

"In what way?"

"She was wearing a fucking turtleneck."

"Are you shitting me?"

"No."

"What'd she say about it?"

"Well, nothing about that specifically, but she's got some stuff going on and she's stressed out about it. She lives with some guy she used to date. Apparently he's kicking her out."

"Sounds like that's probably for the best."

"Yeah, but I still don't like it. I gave her my number, but shit, Dude, I'm still worried about her."

"Want to call Tex to do some recon?"

"Yeah, but I won't."

"Why the hell not? I would. You know I've got Cheyenne monitored 24/7. I won't allow some asshole to take her again."

"I still can't believe you guys got all the women to agree to that shit."

"You don't understand."

Benny nodded. "You're right. I don't, not really. But just because I don't have a woman of my own doesn't mean I don't understand wanting to keep them safe."

"I didn't mean…"

"Yeah, it's okay. I know what you meant. I like Jessyka, Dude. I don't really know her that well, but I'm concerned about her. I don't like that she's living with a guy. I really don't like that she's living with a guy who has given her a deadline to get out of the townhouse they share. I don't like that she feels like she has to stay for his niece who has some self-esteem issues. I don't like that he probably grabbed her and hurt her. And I really don't like that she doesn't have the money to move out."

"What are you doing about it?"

"I don't know."

"Can I give you some advice?"

"Please do. I wouldn't have brought all this shit up if I didn't want your advice, Dude."

"Don't give her space. It sounds like she needs help. If she's as independent as Cheyenne and the other women, she won't reach out. She'll keep on trying to do it all herself. Don't give her a choice."

"What if she gets pissed?"

"Who the fuck cares. She gets pissed, she gets pissed. Then she'll get over it. If it's the right thing to do, and she needs the help, give it to her. Eventually she'll thank you for it."

Benny thought about that for a moment. "You're right."

"Of course I am, Benny-boy."

Benny just rolled his eyes at his friend. "Thanks, man."

"You're welcome. Now go home. My woman is upstairs, and if she's being good, she's doing what I told her to and she's waiting for me just as I asked."

"Jesus, Dude, I don't need to hear this."

Dude just smiled.

"I'm out of here. When you let Cheyenne up for air, thank her for dinner for me."

"Will do."

Now, Benny thought back to the conversation with his friend and knew he had to get on it. He didn't want to wait anymore. He wanted to know how Jess was doing and if she wasn't going to call him, he'd have to go to her.

He stirred the spaghetti sauce on the stove and tested the noodles. They were almost done. Pasta was an easy meal to make for one, and Benny usually had leftovers. He always made the sauce from scratch, there was nothing worse than the bottled crap in the store.

Hearing his phone vibrate, Benny looked over. It was a text from Jess. He smiled and picked up the phone.

I need you.

Benny's muscled clenched immediately. The three words looked so stark on his phone screen. He didn't even hesitate.

Where are you?
Sittig at entrnce to apartmnts
On my way

Benny took the time to turn off the burners, but that was about it. He quickly stuffed his phone in his pocket and headed for the door. He was in his car and headed for Jess's place about thirty seconds after he'd hit the *y* on his last text.

Knowing it was dangerous, but not caring at the moment, he texted Jess back while he drove to her.

Are you ok?

He waited impatiently for her response.

No

Fuck.

Do you need a doctor?
Maybe

Benny pressed his foot down on the gas. Double fuck.

Are you safe where you are?
I think so
Get somewhere where you know you're safe
I don't know where that is anymore
Call me

Fuck the texting thing. Benny needed to hear her voice. His phone rang and Benny put it on speaker as he answered.

"Jess?"

"Yeah, it's me."

Her voice sounded low and scratchy.

"I'm on my way. It'll probably take me another ten minutes. Will you be okay? Should I call an ambulance?"

"No."

"You're scaring the shit out of me, gorgeous. Talk to me."

"Tabitha's gone."

"What do you mean? Who's Tabitha?" Benny didn't like the monotone sound of Jessyka's voice. It sounded like she was in shock.

"She killed herself."

Benny pushed the car a little faster. He was going way over the speed limit, but Jess needed him and he wasn't there.

"Jess…"

"I told her yesterday I was leaving and she killed herself."

It came to Benny suddenly who Tabitha was. Shit. "Why aren't you inside?"

Benny had to figure out what was going on.

"Brian was mad."

Fuck. He knew what was going on now. "Okay, gorgeous. Stay put. I'm coming for you all right? Just hunker down there and I'll be there in a second."

"He…"

"Shhhh," Benny interrupted. He didn't want Jess to relive anything else until he was there with her. "I'll be there in a moment. You can tell me everything when I'm there with you. Just hang on."

"I'm so tired, Kason. You said you were my friend right? I need a friend."

"I'm your friend, Jess. You can rest as soon as I get there. I'll take care of you."

"Okay."

"Go ahead and hang up, Jess, I'm a block away, I'll be there before you know it."

"Okay," she repeated in the same eerie monotone voice she'd been using.

The connection was cut.

Benny clenched his fists around the steering wheel until his fingers turned white. Jesus fuck this was messed up. He felt like he only had snippets of the story, but what he had was bad enough.

He got close to the turn off into Jess's complex when he saw her. She was sitting on the curb, her hands wrapped around her knees and she was leaning over staring at the ground. She didn't move, even when the headlights from his car shone on her. Benny slammed the gearshift into park and got out. He approached Jessyka carefully so as not to startle her.

"Jess?"

Her head whipped up at the sound of his voice and she looked ready to bolt. When she saw it was him she sagged and sighed, "Kason."

Benny didn't hesitate, but went over to her and sat next to her. What he really wanted to do was pick her up and hold her, but until he knew what was wrong and where, and if she was hurt, he couldn't.

Jess's face was tearstained and blotchy from crying. The shirt she was wearing was torn at the neck and was hanging off one shoulder. Benny could see her bra strap highlighted against her shoulder. He couldn't see much more of her than that, but the ripped shirt was enough to make him want to kill someone.

Benny put his hand on the back of Jess's head and held it gingerly. "Where do you hurt, gorgeous?"

"Everywhere."

"I need you to be more specific, Jess. What happened and where did he hurt you?"

Ignoring the first part of his question, she answered the second. "It hurts to breathe. Brian punched me in the stomach. My back hurts because he pushed me and I fell into the corner of the coffee table. My leg hurts because it always hurts when I've pushed it too far. My face hurts because he slapped me a few times and my neck still hurts from the other night." She paused a moment and then said softly, "And my toe hurts because I stubbed it walking over here to sit and text you."

Benny couldn't help but smile at that last part. There was absolutely nothing to smile about, but Jess was so earnest about her poor toe.

"Do you think you can walk to my car?"

Jess looked over at the still-running car sitting about four feet from where they were sitting and said, with a hint of her old spunk, "I think I can manage it."

Benny didn't even smile. "Okay, then up you go. I need to get you out of here." He helped Jess stand up and steadied her when she wobbled. Benny put an arm around her waist and took most of her weight as she hobbled unsteadily to his car. Even though it was only a few feet to the car door, Benny wasn't convinced Jess *could've* made it by herself.

He shut the door and jogged around to the driver's side. Benny had a million questions for her, but he wanted to get her out of there first.

Before he left, Benny leaned over Jessyka and grabbed hold of the seat belt and buckled her in. She hadn't moved since he'd helped her sit, and it was really worrying him.

"Hang in there, Jess."

He watched as she nodded.

Benny tried not to peel out of the parking lot, but he heard the tires squeal as he did a U-turn and turned right toward the emergency room. He wasn't going to take any chances. Jess looked like crap and he didn't like the distant look in her eyes. She said she hurt everywhere, well the doctors could make sure that nothing was broken and that she wasn't bleeding internally. She hadn't said she was assaulted, but maybe she was embarrassed and ashamed about that. Maybe she didn't feel like she knew him well enough to admit it. Just the *thought* of her being hurt that way made his adrenaline spike.

Benny pulled up to the emergency doors and reached over and gently put his hand on Jess's cheek. "We're here."

Her eyes had been closed the entire time they'd been driving, and now she turned her head to look to see where "here" was. Benny watched as her face blanched. "No, please. I don't want to."

"I'll be right here. You have to, Jess. You know it."

She was silent for a moment and when she didn't protest further, Benny knew she was hurting more than just a little bit. He wanted to kill Brian. He didn't know what he looked like, or even where he was at the moment, but he didn't want to kill anyone as badly in his life, as he did Brian right now.

"Come on, gorgeous, let's get you inside."

Benny helped Jess out of the car and when she faltered with her first step, he simply picked her up. He felt something inside him melt when she wrapped her arms around his neck and rested her head on his shoulder.

Benny strode up to the reception desk. "We need a

doctor."

"What's the problem, Sir?" The woman managed to sound business-like and bored at the same time. Benny ground his teeth together.

"The problem is that my friend has had the shit beaten out of her. She's in pain and she needs to be checked out to make sure nothing's fucking broken inside and she isn't going to die of internal bleeding or anything."

Taken aback for a moment, the lady stared at Benny.

Benny felt Jess's hand curl around the back of his neck to try to calm him, and the goose bumps that followed her movement shot all the way down to his toes. That had never happened to him before… and to happen now, in this situation, was almost unbelievable. He tightened his hold on her and held her a little closer.

"Okay, Sir, if you would just follow me down the hall we'll get her settled and a nurse will be in to examine her as soon as possible."

Benny ground his teeth together at her obviously fake polite tone and held Jess tightly as he followed the receptionist down the hall.

He placed Jess on the bed carefully then went to sit in the chair next to it.

The receptionist made a tsking noise and said, "Sorry, Sir, only relatives are allowed to be back here with the patient. You'll have to wait out in the waiting room."

"Oh hell no," Benny said impatiently. "I'm staying." He sat in the chair and reached over to grasp Jess's hand. He kissed the back of it and ignored the sputterings of the woman still trying to get him to leave.

When she finally left, Jess turned to Benny and said with the first hint of a smile he'd seen since he'd found her earlier that night. "You're going to get in trouble."

"I don't care. I'm not leaving."

Five minutes later, a nurse pulled back the curtain and a security guard was standing next to her.

"Sir, you'll have to step out into the waiting area while we take a look at your friend," the nurse explained.

"No."

"Sir…"

Benny broke into her explanation and looked at both her and the security guard as he spoke. "I got a text from my friend, Jess, tonight," he gestured at Jessyka on the bed with his chin and continued. "She said she needed me. She has no immediate family in the area. The girl she loves like a sister killed herself today. Her roommate and ex-boyfriend beat the crap out of her, as you can see. She's in pain and frightened, and she called *me*. I'm a Navy SEAL and I can protect her. I'm not leaving her side. I'll plug my ears and sing a song if there's medical shit you don't want me to hear. I'll do whatever it is you want me to do... except leave."

His voice lowered as he pleaded with the strangers to let him stay. "Please. She needs me."

And she did. They could all see it. Jess's hand was gripping his tightly and she looked between Benny and the security guard apprehensively.

"Ma'am? Do you want him to stay?"

Benny knew they had to ask, but it still pissed him off. He knew they probably thought he was the one who beat her up, but he didn't care. He wasn't leaving, no matter what they thought.

Jessyka obviously knew what they were thinking too. "Yes. God, please, let him stay. I feel safer with him here. If he's here I know Brian can't get to me. Please..."

The nurse glared at Benny. "Okay, but if you cause any problems I'll kick you out so fast you won't know what hit you. Navy SEAL or not."

Benny could only nod jerkily. They were letting him stay. He immediately dismissed the nurse and looked back at Jess. "You're damn right he won't touch you while I'm here. Just relax. They'll make it so you don't hurt anymore and then I'll get you out of here. Hang in there for me."

Benny sat with Jess, while the nurse, then the doctor, examined her. He moved when they told him to, but he never lost touch with Jess. Benny kept a hand on her head, then her arm, then her foot, then back to her head. Wherever the doctor wasn't examining, Benny was there, touching her, reassuring her that she wasn't alone.

Now that they were in the light, Benny got a good look at Jess's neck for the first time. It took all he had not to stalk out of the room and hunt Brian down. She had bruises on her neck in the shape of fingers. The bastard had choked her. It was obvious they were a few days old, so it hadn't been done tonight. No wonder she'd been wearing a turtleneck when he saw her last.

Benny took some deep breaths and tried to stay in the moment. He couldn't go off half-cocked when Jess needed him.

When the doctor was done with the exam, Benny sat in the chair he'd originally been sitting in and took hold of Jess's hand again.

"It looks like nothing is seriously wrong. You were lucky, Jess," the doctor said gently. "Your face will probably bruise and you'll most likely have a black eye. I don't feel any broken ribs or anything. That spot on your back will be painful for a while, but I'll get you some pain killers and if you take it easy for the next couple of days, you'll be able to be up and around with no issues."

"She needs to speak with the police before she goes,"

Benny told the doctor.

Benny thought Jess might protest his words, but she merely nodded as if she'd already resigned herself to the inevitable.

"Okay, I'll be back with the Sergeant and those pain killers I promised. Just relax."

There was silence in the room for a moment after the doctor left. Benny raised the hand that wasn't clutching hers and brushed it lightly over her forehead. Then her cheek. Then her shoulder. Finally, he brushed each bruise on her neck with the back of his hand.

"I wouldn't have let you go back there if I'd known."

Jess obviously was on the same wavelength as he was because she responded, "I know."

"I hate he did this to you."

"I know."

"You're not going back there."

"I know."

Benny smiled for the first time that night. "Is that the only thing you're going to say?"

"Maybe."

He got serious again. "I meant what I said tonight. Brian won't touch you again."

Benny didn't hear her response because a police sergeant entered the little room. For the next thirty minutes Jess rehashed what had happened that night.

Finally when she was done, the cop asked her, "Can I talk to you for a moment alone?"

Benny knew what that meant. Like any good cop, he wanted to make sure Benny didn't have anything to do with what had happened and that it wasn't actually *him* that had beaten Jess up.

Benny saw Jess was about to protest. Needing a moment to get himself together after all he'd heard, Benny stood up and leaned over Jess. He kissed her on the forehead and said softly, but not so softly that the police officer couldn't hear him. "I'll be right outside, gorgeous. No one's getting past me. Okay? Finish up here and we'll leave." He leaned up and met her eyes confidently. Whatever Jess saw in his eyes obviously was enough, because she nodded and said softly, "Okay."

Benny nodded at the officer as he left the room. Doing just as he told Jess he would, he leaned against the wall outside her room and waited. He closed his eyes, hearing her words echo in his mind. He knew he'd never forget them.

"He told me it was my fault."

"He punched me in the stomach and told me I was ugly."

"He wouldn't let go of my throat even though I was gouging my fingernails into his wrist."

"He kicked my hip saying that it wouldn't matter since I was already a cripple."

Benny clenched his teeth and pulled out his phone

and clicked on Wolf's number.

"Hey, Benny."

"Wolf, I have a situation, I need a couple days leave."

Wolf's voice changed from laidback to serious in an instant. "Of course. I'll clear it with the Commander. Anything we can do?"

"Maybe. I'll keep you up to date. Remember Jess, the black haired waitress from the bar?"

"Of course."

"She called me tonight. I'm at the hospital with her and will be taking her back to my place. I know Ice and the others will want to... just give me a couple days before you set them loose on us... okay?"

"Of course. Anything we can do on our side?"

"Yeah, get with Tex on a Brian Thompson." Benny gave Wolf his address. "He beat the shit out of Jess tonight, and apparently has been doing it for a while. He has a sister. Her kid killed herself today."

"Fuck, Benny. Are you sure you don't need us over there?"

"Thanks, man, but I got it. Cops were here tonight, but I don't need that asswipe getting any ideas and deciding to try to get revenge or to try and find Jess."

"We'll take care of it for you. Just call if you need anything else."

"I will. And, Wolf? Thanks."

"Anytime. It's what a team is for."

Benny hung up feeling a bit better, but still way too jacked up. Jess's words still echoing in his brain. *"He kicked me"*... *"He punched me"*... *"He wouldn't let go of my throat"*...

Jess was a hell of a woman, and he knew a lot of strong women. Benny knew Jess wouldn't think that way about herself, but he had to make her see it.

The police officer stuck his head out the door, and seeing Benny standing there, told him he was finished talking with Jessyka. Benny nodded and went back to Jess's side.

After another ten minutes, they were on their way home. The doctor had come in and given Jessyka some pain killers along with a prescription for more if she needed them and a few more warnings to take it easy.

Jess had insisted on walking out on her own, but Benny was right by her side the entire way. They slowly made their way to the waiting area, where Benny, seeing she was fading, plunked her in a chair and ordered in a gentle voice, "Wait here."

Benny knew Jess was still in pain when she didn't argue with him, but only sat where he'd indicated.

He rushed out and got the car he'd had to move earlier, and went back inside to collect Jess. She was sitting on the chair clutching the sides so hard her knuckles were bone white.

"Come on, gorgeous. Let's get out of here."

Benny bent down and gathered Jess into his arms, and he sighed, pleased when she didn't protest.

He strode out of the hospital with Jess in his arms. He settled her into the passenger seat and headed for his apartment.

"What hotel are you taking me to?" Benny heard Jess ask groggily from beside him.

He whipped his head around to look at her incredulously. "You're not going to a fucking hotel. You're coming home with me."

"But, Kason, that's not fair."

"Did you not hear me in the hospital when I said I wasn't leaving your side?"

"Kason, you can't stay with me all the time. I knew you just meant while we were there. And I appreciate it, I do, but this is crazy. You don't know me."

"I wish you'd fucking stop saying that. I know you Jessyka, with a y-k-a, Allen. I know I can't keep you by my side 24/7. It's not practical for either of us. But for the next couple of days I can. We'll talk through what happened with you. We'll talk about Tabitha. You'll cry and let me hold you while you do it and my team will make sure Brian knows he's never to contact you again. Once that's done, we'll figure out what to do about your living situation. But for now you're coming back to my apartment and I don't want to hear anything else about it."

Benny took a deep breath and looked quickly at Jess to see what affect his words had on her. Incredibly she was smiling.

"What are you smiling at?"

"Thank you, Kason. I had no idea where I was going to go tonight. So thank you for taking that burden from me for the moment."

"You're welcome. Now shut your eyes and relax."

"I've heard that before."

"Yeah, well this time when you open them we'll be at my house instead of a park."

Jessyka did as Kason asked, and was asleep within moments.

Chapter Five

J ESS CAME AWAKE slowly. She turned her head and opened her eyes only to see Kason watching her from the driver's seat of the car.

"Oh, are we here?"

"Yeah."

When he didn't say anything else, Jess asked, "Are we going in?"

"Yeah. You just looked so peaceful and relaxed, I didn't want to wake you up." Kason lifted a hand and brushed Jess's hair behind her ear. "Stay put. I'll come around."

Jess could only nod. Kason had a weird look in his eyes. She couldn't really place it, but it looked an awful lot like tenderness. Jess couldn't remember the last time someone had looked at her like that. She liked it a lot.

Kason opened the door for Jess and held her elbow as she got out of the car. He leaned in and grabbed her purse and helped her to his apartment. It was on the lower floor and he had the door opened and her shuttled inside before she could really get a good look around the complex.

"I thought living on the first floor was more dangerous than living on an upper floor?" Jess asked, blurting out her thoughts without really thinking about them. She watched as Kason smiled at her.

"For a single woman? Yeah, it is. For me? Not so much. Besides, I'm not really comfortable living in a building with other people. I don't know what they're doing and if they burn the place down, I want to be able to get out without having to jump off a balcony or something."

"I hadn't thought of that."

Kason laughed and encouraged Jess to keep walking into his apartment with a hand on her lower back, careful to keep away from the large bruise on her back from where she'd been pushed against the coffee table earlier that night.

Jess looked around. Kason's apartment was nothing special. She hated to even think it, but it was true. The walls were white and he had, of course, a giant TV attached to the wall. There was a huge sectional couch with a beat up coffee table sitting in front of it. The kitchen was behind the couch. It was pretty typical for an apartment. Fridge, four burner stove, microwave, dishwasher and a small bar-type counter with two stools. Jess could see two pans sitting on the stove. One had water and noodles in it and the other was filled with some sort of red sauce.

She turned to Kason. "I interrupted your dinner? I'm so sorry!"

"Not a big deal, Jess."

"No, really. I'm sorry."

Kason had gotten Jess to the sectional and he helped her ease down into it. He'd placed her in the middle of one of the sides and after she'd sat down, he picked her feet up and swung them on the cushions.

Without a word he unlaced both shoes and put them on the floor, under the coffee table, out of the way. Benny grabbed a throw pillow from the side of the couch and helped arrange it under Jess's head. Once he was done, Benny leaned in and put his hands on either side of her. His voice was low and controlled.

"I don't give a fuck about dinner. I can re-make dinner. I can't re-make you, Jess. So yeah, if you text me and say you need me, I don't care what I'm doing, I'll always drop it and come to you." He paused, as if he was letting his words sink in. "Got it?"

Jess could only nod. She wasn't sure she *did* get it, but it was obvious Kason had strong feelings on the subject, so she let it go.

"Are you hungry?"

Jess shook her head.

"Are you in pain? Can I get you anything?"

Jess shook her head again.

"Okay, get comfortable. I'll be right back."

Jess watched as Kason stood up and headed down a hallway off of the living room. She closed her eyes, trying desperately to stay in the moment and not let her mind go back to what had happened that night.

Kason was back a couple of minutes later. He was now dressed in a pair of badly cut off sweat pants and a T-shirt that looked like it had been in its prime about twenty years ago. His feet were bare and his hair was mussed, as if he'd run his fingers through it a few times. He was carrying two pillows and a fuzzy blanket. He put them on top of the coffee table and went into the kitchen, still without a word.

Jess heard the faucet running and the refrigerator opening. Kason came back around the couch and she could see he was carrying two glasses of water. He put them on the coffee table as well. Then he turned and looked down at her as if trying to decide where to sit. Finally he went to her head and gently lifted the pillow so he could sit down. Then he propped the pillow on his leg and gently eased Jess's head back down. Benny's hand came to rest on her forehead and stayed there. Every now and then his thumb would move in a small caress over her hairline, but otherwise he was still.

When he didn't say anything, Jess looked up at him. Kason had his head tipped back so it was resting on the back of the couch with his eyes closed.

"Kason?"

"Yeah, Jess?"

"Are you okay?"

His head came up and he looked down at her. "Yeah. I'm okay. I'm just so relieved you're here and that bastard didn't hurt you any worse than he did. I'm trying to come up with a way to have you talk to me about what happened where you don't have to re-live it all, but I'm not having any luck."

Jess closed her eyes at Benny's words and said in a small voice, "Do I have to talk about it?"

"Yeah, I think you do. Jess, look at me."

Jess took a deep breath and opened her eyes. Kason was leaning over her now, one hand had moved to her cheek and just laid there, the other he put on her stomach.

"I've been there, gorgeous. Not exactly where you are, but I've been captured while on a mission. We were... asked... to give up information... but we wouldn't. I had a cousin who killed himself too. Cookie's woman lived through Hell after being kidnapped by sex traffickers down in Mexico... and she had a breakdown because she didn't talk about it with anyone.

"I've been there, Jess. I know how important it is to talk it out. I'm probably not the best person you can talk to, but I'm here now and I'm your friend. Talk to me. Tell me what happened. Get it out. Then tomorrow in the light of day, we can start to figure out where to go from here. But for now, here tonight, let me have it. I'm your friend, Jess. Give it to me."

Jess scrunched her eyes closed. "I-I…"

Before she could finish her sentence, even though she didn't really know what she was going to say, Kason was moving. He stood up and encouraged Jess to sit up as well. He sat on the other side of her, then lay down so his back was to the back of the couch. He pulled Jess down until she was lying in front of him. Her back to his stomach. He curled one arm around her waist and pulled her back until she was completely surrounded by him.

"Am I hurting you?"

"No," Jess whispered back, even though every time she moved she *did* hurt. She closed her eyes again. She curled her arms up until they were in front of her and her hands were resting under her cheek. She could feel every inch of Kason behind her. His legs were bent, as were hers, and they were touching from her feet to her head. The warmth of his body seeped into hers as if he was her own personal electric blanket. She hadn't realized until that moment how cold she'd been. She shivered.

Kason leaned over her and snagged the blanket from the coffee table. He awkwardly spread it over their bodies, carefully tucking it in around Jess so that every inch of her body was covered. He lay back down and Jess felt his lips on the top of her head.

Jess could feel Kason waiting. "I don't know where to start," she told him honestly. So much was running through her head she didn't know how to tell him anything.

"Take your time. I'm not going anywhere. Start wherever seems right."

After a few moments, Jess started.

"I met Tabitha when she was ten. She was overweight and sad. I could see the sadness right away. But she was so smart. She could write stories that made me cry. At ten, Kason. She was that good. Her mom worked two jobs, so she was never home. Brian... well, he wasn't much of an uncle. I tried to make up for it. I'd take her places, we'd go exploring. We'd laugh, we'd have a good time. Every time when I dropped her off back at her place, she'd be happy. Then the next time I'd see her, I'd have to cheer her up all over again. This happened over and over. All the time. As she got older she retreated into herself even more. I tried to help. I tried to talk to Tammy about it, but she just got mad at me. I tried to talk to Brian, but he told me he didn't care. That Tabitha was fat and ugly and I might as well not bother."

Jess took a breath and felt Kason's hand rubbing up

and down the side of her body. It was rhythmic and soothing. He hadn't interrupted her to ask questions, he was just listening. It felt good.

"It was earlier this year that Brian started getting physical with me. I always knew he had a temper, but after we broke up and were just friends, he seemed to have a handle on it. That's why I moved in. He was more like the fun-loving guy I knew in high school. I don't know what happened. Something *had* to have happened. It was like a switch went off in him. One day he was laughing with me over me spilling something in the kitchen and the next day he was grabbing my arm and flinging me across the kitchen telling me I was a worthless cripple."

"Drugs."

"What?"

"Drugs. It's the only thing I can think of that would make his personality change so drastically like that," Benny said in a low confident voice.

Jess thought about it. Kason was probably right. She didn't know who Brian was hanging out with at the construction site, but something had to have triggered his change in personality. Drugs made as much sense as anything else.

"I hadn't thought it could be drugs affecting him," Jess said. "Whatever it was, it scared me. But when Brian started belittling Tabitha when she was visiting, I knew I couldn't bring her there anymore. I was scared for her. I was scared for me. I didn't know what to do. I wanted to get out. I'm not an idiot, Kason, I swear I'm not. I *knew* I shouldn't stay with someone who was hitting me, but if I left, Tabitha wouldn't have anyone on her side. I struggled with it for a while."

"I know. I could see your struggle when we came into *Aces*."

Jess nodded against Kason, but fell silent.

"What happened tonight?"

"I knew I had to get out. If Brian had no problem choking me, how far would he go? I knew I couldn't stay until the end of the month, even if that meant I wouldn't get to see Tabitha. I contacted a women's shelter and they said they'd take me for a while until I could get the money to get my own place."

Jess felt Kason's muscles clench behind her. The arm around her waist tightened a fraction. She could feel him consciously loosen his grip on her.

When she didn't continue, Kason urged, "Go on."

"So I got some of my stuff together and put it by the door. I went over to talk to Tabitha. Tammy was out, so we stayed in and I talked to her for an hour. I explained what happened with Brian and why I was leaving. I told her I wasn't leaving *her*, but I couldn't live with Brian anymore. I warned her about him. Told her not to listen to anything he said to her, that she was a beautiful person inside and out." Jess's breath hitched and she forced back a sob. She had to get through this.

"She hugged me and told me not to worry about her, that she'd be okay. We both cried a little bit. She gave me a copy of the newest story she'd written. I felt pretty good about it when I left. I'd been so scared to tell her, but Tabitha was strong. She was encouraging and said she understood. But Kason... she didn't. She was lying."

"It's okay, Jess, I've got you. Finish it."

Jess could feel Kason's arms tighten around her. She burrowed further into the blanket and his arms.

"A little while later, I'd arrived home when Brian came in. I was getting the last of my stuff together and he slammed the door open. He came right up to me and punched me in the stomach without saying anything. I fell back against the coffee table and he ranted at me. He screamed that Tabitha was dead. That she'd taken a bunch of pills and was dead. There wasn't a note or anything, but I know why she did it."

"No, Jess. You will not take this on yourself. I won't let you," Benny said firmly.

"But Kason..."

"No. You did nothing wrong. You didn't kill her. She was a fourteen year-old teenager, whose mother didn't take care of her emotionally. She was overweight and probably picked on at school. She was a loner who didn't have any friends. She was the creative type. I could go on and on, but your words to her today did *not* make her do this. She obviously had it already planned. Think about it for a second."

Jess didn't want to think about it. Kason continued anyway, even when Jess shook her head.

"Maybe she was hanging on for *you*. Maybe she was just existing in her life as you were in yours, because she was worried about you. Once she knew you'd be okay, and were getting out, she felt free to do what she felt she had to do. I'm not condoning it. I don't think anyone should end their life in order to escape emotional issues, but Jess, you can't blame yourself. You're a victim here too."

Jess couldn't speak. It just hurt too badly.

"Turn over, gorgeous, let me hold you."

Jess awkwardly turned around in Kason's arms until she was facing him. She buried her head into his chest and sniffled.

"Finish it, Jess. What else did Brian do?" Benny knew. He'd heard the story as she told it to the officer in the hospital, but he wanted her to get it all out here and now, safe in his arms.

"Nothing he hadn't already done before. He called me a cripple. Made fun of me. Kicked me, smacked me around, then threw me against the wall. He said if I was leaving to get the hell out. I didn't hesitate. I just grabbed my purse and left. I don't have any of my stuff. I don't have anything."

"You'll get your stuff, Jess. Don't worry about that. I'll take care of it. And you have something. You have me. I'm your friend. I have your back. You don't have to go to the women's shelter. I have two bedrooms. It's a crappy apartment, but you aren't homeless. You can stay here as long as it takes to save up enough money for a place of your own."

At Kason's words, Jess burst into tears. She couldn't hold them back anymore. Kason didn't tell her to hush, he didn't tell her it would all be okay, he just held her. He rocked her and ran his hands up and down her back.

Jess had no idea how long she'd been crying when she finally found herself out of tears. She was exhausted, completely drained. She opened her eyes and saw she'd soaked Kason's shirt.

"I got you all wet."

Kason chuckled above her. "I've slogged through the pits of hell on missions. I survived Hell Week. I've trudged through jungles without a shower for a week. A few tears and some snot doesn't bother me in the least."

His words made Jess blush. She hadn't even thought about snot! "Jesus. Well, I'm sorry anyway, this isn't the jungle or Hell Week."

She could feel the chuckle rumble through Kason's chest. It felt nice.

"Do you want some water or anything?"

Jess shook her head. She was comfortable right where she was. "I don't want to move."

"Okay." Jess felt Kason's hand on the back of her head. He pressed until her cheek was once more resting on his chest. "Go to sleep. We'll figure things out in the morning."

"But…"

"Jess, I'm tired. You're tired. It's been a hell of a day. Just relax. Trust me. I've got you. You're safe, just sleep."

"Okay." Jess paused then quickly said, "Thank you. For everything."

"You're welcome, Jess. Thank *you* for contacting me. It means a lot. Sleep now."

Jessyka didn't think she'd be able to sleep, but surprisingly, she was out of it within moments. She never knew that Kason stayed awake for another hour, simply enjoying the feel of her in his arms. She never heard him mutter softly, "You'll always be safe if I have anything to say about it."

Chapter Six

BENNY TRIED TO be quiet in the kitchen as he fixed Jessyka a good hearty breakfast. He was still going through all she'd told him last night. He had a lot of work to do in order to help her, but first he wanted to get some food into her.

All his life, Benny had felt a need to protect people, but his thoughts about Jess were way beyond anything he'd ever felt before. He'd been a horndog in the past, sleeping with women for a night and then not thinking twice about how they were feeling when he never called them again. But Benny had never found anyone who he actually liked. Who he wanted to get to know outside the bedroom. But with Jess, he found that he wanted to know everything about her. He wanted to know who her friends were, her favorite foods, her everyday routine, just everything.

Benny had never been friends with a woman before. He supposed it was cliché, but there it was. He used women and they used him. Now that he thought about it, he was friends with his teammates' women, but that was different somehow. They were already taken. There was no chance of them wanting to be in his bed, and he certainly didn't want to be in theirs. But Jess? Yeah, Benny could admit he wanted her in his bed, but along with that was the fact that he just plain liked her. She was strong, hardworking, witty, and she was compassionate. She didn't look at him and see a conquest. At least he didn't think she did.

He knew Jess was different when the thought of her in his kitchen didn't freak him out. He didn't like when people tried to "help" him when he was cooking. He was meticulous about it, and had been made fun of on more than one occasion by his teammates and their women, but it was just the way he was.

The first thing he'd thought of this morning was a vision of Jess standing next to him as they fixed breakfast together. Benny supposed it was partly because he'd held her all night. The feel of her body next to his was unlike anything he'd felt before. In the past he'd cuddle with a woman because it was expected of him after sex, not because he felt any real connection with her. That probably made him an asshole, but he couldn't force feelings when there weren't any there.

But with Jess, Benny had been completely satisfied holding her all night. He didn't feel the urge to have sex with her, he just wanted to hold her and make sure she felt safe.

Benny was brought out of his musings when he saw Jessyka's head pop up from over the couch.

"Sleep well?" he called out, stirring the eggs in the bowl he was holding.

Jess turned her head and saw him in the kitchen. "Surprisingly, yeah."

"I've got an extra toothbrush and toothpaste in the bathroom. I don't have any girly soap or shampoo, but you can use mine if you want to shower." Benny watched as Jess's eyes got big. Yeah, she wanted to shower.

"Clothes will be an issue until Dude gets here this morning with your stuff, but in the meantime, I put one of my shirts in the bathroom along with a pair of boxers. They'll be big on you, but they'll do until later."

Jess blushed, hoping Kason couldn't see it. Just the *thought* of wearing his underwear made goosebumps break out all over her body. She tried to tamp down her reaction. Kason was her friend, no matter how sexy he was, she didn't want to ruin the best thing to happen to her in the last year.

"I'd love a shower, thanks." She stood up and swayed a bit, catching herself on the couch.

Before she could take a step, Kason was there with a hand on her elbow, steadying her.

"Are you okay? I should've asked that first."

"I'm good. I just stood up too fast."

"How's the hip?"

"Kason, I'm okay. I promise." Jess watched as he backed off, still looking worried.

"If you don't mind, take a few steps so I know you won't face plant on my floor the second I turn my back," Benny demanded, wanting to see for himself that Jess could walk.

He watched as Jess did as he asked. She looked okay, she had her normal limp, but it didn't look any more exaggerated than he'd seen it before. He headed back to the kitchen and the words popped out before he could stop them.

"Brian's a fucking idiot. You're not crippled. I love your gait." Benny watched as Jess turned to him with an incredulous look on her face. He decided to play it off as nonchalantly as he could. Sometime between his making breakfast for her and coming to her side to make sure she didn't hurt herself, he'd decided she was his. Benny couldn't have all these protective feelings about her and not want to keep her. He'd give her as much time as she needed, but he hoped in the end, whenever that might be, she'd want to keep him right back.

"I don't know why you have that limp, but I'm assuming somehow your left leg is shorter than the other. I've watched you for several months now. Jess, it's sexy as hell. You don't get that, but I do, and so do my teammates. When you walk, you sway. Because of the difference in the length of your legs, your hips have an exaggerated back and forth movement to them. From behind, your ass just begs to be caressed. From the front, your sway makes your breasts move with your body. Again, it's sexy as all hell. For Brian to call you crippled just means he doesn't appreciate the female form. And Jess, your form is abso-fucking-lutely perfect. Own it, because I swear to God, every man in that bar appreciates it. Swear to fucking God."

Jess stood in the entrance to the hallway that apparently led to the bedrooms and bathroom. She simply stared at Benny, not knowing what, if anything, she was supposed to say to him.

Benny smiled and continued to beat the eggs, getting them just the right consistency before he poured them into the pan to make an omelet. He'd gotten to her, as he'd meant to, but every word out of his mouth had been the truth. It was time she stopped believing the words that asshole spewed to her for too damn long.

"You taking that shower, gorgeous, or are you just going to stand there staring at me?"

Jess turned and fled down the hallway, ignoring Benny's laugh as she hurried away.

Thirty minutes later Benny heard the bathroom door open. He turned to the hallway and waited for Jess to appear.

She walked into the living area of the apartment and he could only stare at her. Her black hair looked shiny and clean and he could smell the scent of his soap wafting out into the room. But what really caught his attention was her body. Jess was wearing his clothes and that made his heart beat faster.

She walked slowly over to the stools at the bar counter and pulled herself up. Benny could see more of her body than he'd seen in a long time. The boxers left her legs bare and the shirt covered most of her upper arms, but her forearms were exposed. The shirt was also big enough that it kept falling off one shoulder. He watched as she hitched it up with her hand as she sat.

Benny clenched his fists and tried to calm himself down. The bruises on her forearms were highly visible against her pale skin. The marks at her throat were fading, but it was obvious what they were as well. He hadn't gotten a good look at her legs before she'd sat, but Benny knew he'd see bruises there too.

He turned to the stove and poured the egg mixture into the steaming pan. "I hope an omelet is okay for breakfast." Benny thought he sounded pretty normal, especially for the murderous thoughts that were coursing through his brain.

"It's more than okay. I haven't had an omelet in forever. Thank you, Kason."

"You don't have to thank me for every single thing I

do, Jess."

"I feel like I do."

"Well, you don't. You are *not* a guest in this house. You live here too. I'm sure you'll do your part as well. Think how annoying it'll be if we go around thanking each other all the time." Benny tried to lessen the blow of his words by smiling.

Jess grinned back. "Okay. I'll try. I'm just not used to anyone doing anything for me like this. Brian never did."

"Well, one, I'm definitely not Brian. And two, you better get used to it."

It was obvious Jess was going to ignore his words from earlier, and that was okay with Benny. He didn't want to rush her, but he'd do whatever he could, say whatever he needed to say, to erase the hurtful words she'd most likely heard too many times from the jerk she'd lived with.

He put a glass of orange juice in front of her and turned back to the stove to flip the eggs.

"What time do you go into work?" Jess asked.

Benny turned back to her resting his palms on the edge of the counter behind him. "I'm not going to work for a couple of days. I'm taking some leave."

"You can't do that."

"Why not?"

"Well... because."

Benny laughed at her. "That's not an answer. Look. You can't possibly think I'm going to just leave you here by yourself the day after I took you to the emergency room do you?"

"Uh…"

"Not happening, Jess. We've got shit we have to do. First up, Dude'll be bringing some of your stuff over. At some point we have to go over there and get the rest of your things packed. I'm not letting you go back there without me or one of the guys with you. We need to find out the details of the funeral for Tabitha. I won't allow you to be harangued by Tammy or Brian, so if I need to arrange a time for you to say your good-bye to Tabitha in person, that's what I'll do. You need to call the women's shelter and tell them you won't need the room you arranged with them. You also need to talk to your boss and tell him what's going on and figure out your work schedule. On top of all that, the girls will want to come over and see for themselves that you're okay. I've bought you some time with that, but I expect that will only last for a day or two, so you have to brace for the onslaught."

"I don't understand," Jess whispered, completely overwhelmed.

"What don't you understand?" Benny came over to the bar and leaned on it, giving Jess his complete attention.

"I can do all those things, you don't have to stay home from work."

"Jess, it's what friends do for each other. You aren't alone anymore. I've got your back. My friends have your back."

"I don't think it's what friends do. I mean, I've never had friends that have done anything like this before."

Benny reached over the bar and put his palm on Jess's cheek. "You have friends that do that kind of thing now, gorgeous."

Jess couldn't help it, she leaned her head to the side and brought her hand up and put it over his on her face. "Thank you," she whispered.

Smiling, Benny teased, "What did I tell you about saying 'thank you' all the time?" He put his other hand on the back of her neck and pulled her gently across the bar, kissed her on the top of the head then let go. "Do you need to take a pain pill?"

Jess had only a moment to feel disappointed Kason had removed his hands before he'd changed the subject. She thought about it for a moment. "No, I think I'm all right." At Kason's frown, she quickly added, "But if I hurt later, I'll take one. Promise."

"Okay, I was just going to suggest that it might be good if you took it with food. Here you go, omelet with tomatoes, green peppers, onions, red peppers, chorizo sausage, a little bit of bacon, and of course topped with a ton of shredded cheese. I have sour cream and salsa if you want to add a southwest flair to it."

"Are you shitting me?"

"Nope, dig in."

"I've never met a man who can cook."

"Well, you've met one now. Eat."

Jess picked up the fork and looked up at Kason. "What are you eating?"

"Mine's cooking now."

"I'll wait." Jess put down her fork.

"No you won't. Eat, Jess. It'll get cold. Mine won't take long."

"But that's rude," she pouted.

Benny laughed. God, she was cute. "No, it's not. Not if I tell you to eat. Do it. Seriously, it's much better when it's still hot."

"Oh all right. But next time *you* eat first."

Benny wasn't going to agree with Jess, but he smiled at her anyway. He was glad to see her in a relatively good mood. Benny had no idea what her frame of mind was going to be when she got up that morning. She had a hard day yesterday and she was going to have another few tough days. Jess would never completely be able to put the loss of Tabitha behind her, but maybe, just maybe with a little luck and a lot of support, she could deal with it and move on.

Benny agreed with her last statement about eating

first, knowing he lied as he said it. "Okay, Jess, next time I'll eat first." He watched with satisfaction as she closed her eyes and groaned as she chewed the first bite of the omelet. Amazingly, Benny felt himself grow hard. Fuck. He had to control himself. He didn't want to scare her away. He turned back to the stove.

"Jesus, Kason. This is awesome."

Benny shrugged. "It's just an omelet."

"Uh, no. It's not. It's... hell, I don't have the words, but I'm sure if you were on one of those cooking reality shows you'd win hands down."

"Thanks, I think. Now quit talking and eat."

Jess just shook her head at him and did as he requested.

Not long after they'd finished breakfast and Jess had done the dishes, at her insistence, there was a knock at the door.

"Stay put, I'll get it," Benny said.

Jess knew it was an order, even though he'd used a gentle tone. She stood next to the bar by the kitchen and waited to see who it was. Benny opened the door and one of his military friends came in.

"Hey, Dude, Thanks for coming over. Did you have any issues?"

"Nope, didn't see anyone. Just got in and grabbed the bag. It was right where you said it would probably be."

The man turned his piercing eyes onto Jess. She felt completely naked standing in the room in nothing but Kason's shirt and boxers, but forced herself to come forward and thank the big man for bringing her bag over. "Thank you so much!"

"Are you fucking shitting me?"

Jess was taken aback at the harsh words coming out of Benny's friend's mouth and involuntarily took a step away from him.

"Dude..." Benny warned in a quiet voice.

"You didn't tell me he tried to fucking choke her, Benny."

Jess brought her hand up to her throat and tried to cover the lingering marks. She'd honestly forgotten about them. Benny had made her feel so comfortable and relaxed around him, she hadn't even remembered her bruises.

"I told you there was a reason she was wearing a tur-tleneck."

"The only reason a woman should feel obligated to wear a fucking turtleneck when it's seventy fucking degrees outside is if she needs to cover up the angry marks a man made on her neck the night before because she doesn't want anyone to see and because some asshat guy doesn't want anyone to ask any questions and get his ass thrown in jail."

Holy crap. His words made Jess shift where she was

standing. This guy was intense, but he hadn't made a move toward her and his words came off as concerned somehow at the same time being very scary. It was obvious he was pissed at Brian, not her. She'd sensed he was somehow more intense than the other men that she'd met at *Aces*, but up close, he was kinda scaring the shit out of her.

Dude continued his mini-tirade. "You having those marks on your neck means that asshole you lived with needs a lesson in manners and the proper way to treat a woman." Dude walked further into the apartment and came to Jess.

Jessyka's eyes moved to Kason. He said he wouldn't let anyone hurt her. She couldn't run, for one, her hip wouldn't allow it, but two, she had nowhere to go in the small space. She took a breath. Kason looked calm. Whatever his friend wanted with her, it wasn't to hurt her. His non-concern about his friend hurting her allowed her to have the courage to stay where she was as the big SEAL came toward her.

Dude gently took her chin in his hand and raised her head. Jess felt his other hand brush against her neck. Then he dropped her chin and picked up one of her hands, he pushed the sleeve of her shirt up to examine the bruises on her upper arm, then did the same on the other side. "He cause that limp?"

Jess shook her head, she couldn't get a word out of

her tight throat if her life depended on it.

Dude cocked his head as if determining if she was telling the truth or not. Whatever he saw apparently was enough, because he turned on his heel and headed back to the door. "I'm calling Wolf. We'll get the rest of her shit today. You take care of her." Then he was out the door and gone.

Jess let out a breath and looked at Kason again. He was standing at the now closed door.

"Come here."

Jess didn't think. She went to him. She limped across the room and straight into Kason's arms. As they closed around her, she breathed easy for the first time since the knock on the door happened.

"He's a little intense," Jess commented, even if it felt like the understatement of the year.

Benny laughed. "You don't know the half of it. You okay? Dude would never hurt you, but you didn't know that."

"I *did* know it. Okay, well, not at first, but you said you wouldn't let anyone hurt me and you didn't move when he came toward me, so I figured I was okay."

"Jesus, Jess. Thank you for trusting me."

"I thought we weren't supposed to thank each other," Jess said with a grin, looking up at Kason as he held her in the circle of his arms.

He laughed. "You got me there. Okay, let's tackle one thing at a time today. Go get dressed. I'm assuming you have some clothes in the bag Dude brought." Benny gestured to the bag sitting on the floor that Dude had dropped by the door when he'd stalked inside.

"Once you're dressed, we'll handle the other shit. Obviously we can cross 'getting your stuff' off the list, Dude and the guys have that covered."

"How will they know what's mine and what's Brian's?"

"They'll figure it out, and if they don't, who fucking cares. If they miss anything, I'll get it for you."

"I can't ask you to…"

"You didn't ask. I offered." Benny interrupted Jess before she could finish her thought and leaned down, grabbed her bag and handed it to her. "Now get changed. As much as I like seeing you in my shirt, we have shit we have to do, and I'm not letting you leave the apartment looking like sex on a stick. Get moving." Benny let go of Jess and turned her gently to face the room. He gave her a little push to the small of her back.

"You guys must take lessons in 'bossy,'" Jess said, laughing as she limped toward the hallway. She looked back to see Kason's eyes on her ass as she walked. She faltered a bit remembering what he'd told her earlier.

She watched as Benny's eyes came up off her ass and up to meet her eyes. He merely winked and dropped his eyes again. Jess could only laugh and shake her head as she limped out of sight down the hallway.

Chapter Seven

JESSYKA SAT ON the couch at Kason's apartment and tried not to cry. She'd cried enough for one day.

While the morning had started off all right, the rest of the day had sucked. She'd called her boss at the bar and he'd been horrified at everything that had happened. Luckily, since she was a good employee, he'd given her an entire week off.

Next, Jess had contacted the women's shelter and let them know she was safe and with a friend. Jess loved how Kason had put his hand over hers when she'd said that.

Then Kason took over and called Wolf. Dude had already talked to him and the rest of the SEAL team had arranged to go over to her old place and collect her belongings. Caroline, who was apparently married to Wolf, insisted on accompanying them. Jess had wanted to go too, but Kason waved her off and continued making arrangements without her involvement.

Jess had been pissed, but after Kason had explained

that she had to go and see about Tabitha, she relented. He was right. If his friends could go over and get her things without her, why shouldn't she let them? Deep down inside she was relieved she wouldn't have to face Brian or the townhouse where she had such horrible memories again.

The last thing on the list was Tabitha and the reason the rest of the day had sucked. Kason had pulled some strings and talked to the caretaker of the funeral home. The guy had explained that Tammy had requested to have Tabitha's body cremated. She hadn't even arranged a service for her daughter.

Kason arranged for Jessyka to be able to go and say her goodbyes. Jess had no idea how he'd done it... surely it wasn't as easy as calling up and saying they wanted to see a body... she technically wasn't even related to Tabitha... but somehow Kason had done it. They'd arrived at the funeral home that afternoon. The caretaker had led them to a back room and left them alone with Tabitha's body.

Jess had stood paralyzed by the door, staring at the gurney. She knew Tabitha lay under the sheet and she didn't know if she could handle seeing her.

"I can't," she said quietly, her voice hitching.

"Take your time, Jess." Kason wrapped his arms around her from behind and pulled her into his body. She melted into him, desperate for some support.

"I can't," she repeated despondently.

"Okay."

Jess didn't move and neither did Kason.

After what seemed like forever, but was probably only a minute or two, Jess took a hesitant step toward the body on the platform, then stopped. The sheet was almost obscenely white. She wished like hell Tabitha would sit up suddenly and say "surprise!" and giggle the way Jess remembered she used to do when she was younger.

"What if she doesn't look like Tabitha? I can't have my last glimpse of her that way."

"Stay here." Kason put his hands on her shoulders and pressed down. He leaned down and spoke quietly into Jess's ear. "I'll take a look and let you know. Do you trust me?"

"Yes." Jessyka's answer was immediate and relieved. "I shouldn't ask you to…"

"Jess, look at me." Benny came around her and stood in front of her, blocking her view of the body under the sheet. He put his finger under her chin. "I can handle this. I'm a SEAL. This won't be the first dead person I've seen. Okay? Trust me to know if you can handle this."

Jess could only nod. She briefly leaned forward and put her forehead on Kason's chest, needing that contact. Her hands came to his sides and gripped his T-shirt in her fists. She felt Kason's hands come around her and enfold her into his body. They stood like that for a minute or so, then she felt Kason's arms loosen. He kissed the top of her head and then gently spun her around so she was looking at the door.

"Give me a second."

Jess simply nodded again. She heard the rustle of the sheet and then nothing. Then Kason was back.

"It's okay, come on."

Jess took a deep breath and turned around. Kason put his arm around her and they walked to Tabitha's side together.

Kason had pulled the sheet down enough so Tabitha's face was the only thing visible. Jess choked back a sob. It looked like she was sleeping. Tabitha was pale, but otherwise she looked just like she had the last time Jess had seen her.

Jess lost it. She didn't think she'd ever cried that hard. Kason had been so patient and kind with her too. He'd held her and murmured words of encouragement. He hadn't rushed her, as a lot of men might have. Jess thought they were in the room for at least an hour. Every time Jess had decided she was ready to go, she couldn't make herself leave.

Finally she was ready. Jess thought she'd gone through all five stages of grief in that hour with Tabitha. First she had tried to deny she was really dead. Tabitha had looked so normal, that she hadn't believed she could be dead at first. Then she'd gotten mad. Tabitha had no right to kill herself. It was selfish and inconsiderate of their friendship. Then Jess had moved to the bargaining stage. Kason had to reel her back in from that one. She'd gone back to the "if only" statements she'd made the night before. Kason gently reminded her that it wasn't her fault and there wasn't anything Jess could have done to make the outcome any different.

Finally she cried. Hard. It was depressing as hell to see such a wonderful person, lifeless. The world would never get to read her wonderful stories, they'd never get to see what an awesome person Tabitha was. Finally, Jess had moved to acceptance. Tabitha was dead. She wasn't in pain anymore. Jess didn't have to worry about her friend being overly sensitive to everyday life events.

Jess knew she'd revisit all of the same feelings she'd just gone through sooner rather than later though. An hour wasn't enough to completely heal, but she knew she felt as okay as she did, because Kason was there with her.

Jess had kissed Tabitha on the forehead, crying a bit again, feeling the coldness of her skin, and finally let Kason tug the sheet back up and over Tabitha's face.

"Come on, gorgeous, let's get out of here."

Jess had nodded and they'd left. Kason thanked the caretaker and he'd taken them to the same park he'd pulled into not too long ago when he was taking her home from work that first night. He hadn't said anything, but just helped her out of the car and they'd made the short walk to a bench. They'd sat on the bench and talked about Tabitha, and about nothing important for over two hours. Finally, after Jess's stomach had growled, Kason had helped her up and taken her back to his car and back to his apartment.

Now she was sitting on his couch, comfortable and warm, and trying not to cry. Jess felt like she'd been crying all day. She hated being such a wimp, she'd never been one to feel sorry for herself. She needed a distraction. She got up and made her way to the kitchen.

"Can I help?"

Benny looked up at Jessyka. She'd been strong all day and he was so proud of her. He wanted to make a good home-style meal for her. He'd never invited a woman to assist him in the kitchen before. It was his space, the place he went when he needed to decompress. But the thought of having Jess standing next to him helping him, felt right. It felt like the next natural step in their relationship... whatever that was.

"I'd like nothing more than for you to help me, Jess."

Jessyka tilted her head, somehow knowing there was more to his words than she was understanding, but she wasn't feeling up to figuring it out right now.

"Where do you want me?"

Benny chuckled, if Jess knew where he really wanted her, she'd probably run screaming from the apartment.

"Come'ere. You chop the veggies while I put together the lasagna."

"You're making lasagna? Isn't that… complicated?"

Benny leaned toward Jess and got in her space. "What? You don't think I can do complicated?"

Jess swallowed hard. There were times when she thought Kason wanted more from her than just friendship, like now, but then other times he acted just like a buddy, like a friend would. "I-I-I'm sure you can." She hated how her voice stuttered.

"I can do complicated, gorgeous. Promise. I like to cook. I'm good at it. This is gonna be the best lasagna you've ever eaten."

"If the omelet this morning was any indication, I'm sure it will be."

They worked around each other in the small space. Jess would reach for a knife around Kason as he worked on layering the sauce and noodles in the pan. He would stretch over her and snatch a slice of green pepper off of the cutting board as she chopped. They laughed and joked with each other. It was just what Jess needed. She felt normal.

"Here, taste this."

Jess turned to see Kason holding a wooden spoon

out to her with a dollop of sauce on it. He had one hand under the spoon to catch any sauce that might drip. "Guarantee it's the best sauce you've ever tasted."

Without thinking, Jess took hold of Kason's wrist on the hand that was holding the spoon and leaned toward him. She opened her mouth and looked up at him just as she closed her lips around the spoon. She almost choked at the heat pouring out of his eyes. She pulled back and licked her lips, letting go of his wrist.

"Good, isn't it?" Benny asked, not taking his eyes off of Jess's lips. He took his thumb and wiped the corner of her mouth where some errant sauce lingered. He suppressed his groan as her tongue came out and licked right where he'd just been touching.

"Jesus, Kason, that *is* the best thing I've ever tasted."

Her innocent words made Benny's libido sit up and take notice... again. She hadn't meant anything by what she'd said, but his mind immediately went into the gutter. Her words accompanied by the visual of how she'd opened her mouth, held on to his wrist and how her eyes looked up at him with open honesty and anticipation, made him immediately harden in his jeans. He knew she'd look exactly like that kneeling at his feet as she prepared to take him into her mouth.

"Just wait until you taste the finished product, gorgeous," Benny managed, keeping his lower body turned away from her, swallowing hard, trying to remember the tough day she'd had. She didn't need to deal with his obvious desire on top of everything else.

After Benny put the lasagna into the oven to cook, he suggested they eat the salad while they were waiting for the main dish. He could hear Jess's stomach growling and didn't want her to have to wait another hour to eat. They sat at the bar and munched on the salad. They talked about nothing important, until Benny saw some of the sadness lift from Jess's eyes.

The only thing that happened while they were eating that Benny didn't like, was when he reached across the bar for the salt shaker. Jess had startled and almost fallen off her stool trying to get away from his reaching arm.

Benny had stopped immediately and looked at her in concern. "Just getting the salt, Jess," he soothed.

"Yeah, I know… sorry." She blushed in embarrassment and wouldn't meet his eyes.

Kason put his hand on her forearm lightly and stroked her with his thumb as he spoke. "Don't be sorry, but I hope you *do* know you have nothing to be afraid of with me or with any of my teammates. We might be big and mean, but you are *never* in danger of being hurt or hit when we're around."

"I know Kason. I *know*. I just… it's just instinctive. You can't erase years of me being cautious in one night. Just be patient with me."

Slowly Benny brought his hand up to Jess's cheek. "As long as you know you're safe, I'll try to be patient."

"I know I'm safe."

"Okay then, will you please pass the salt? I should've asked in the first place instead of being rude and reaching for it. My mom would've smacked the back of my head if she'd been here." He smiled at her, lightening the mood once again.

Jessyka laughed and shook her head. Kason never did what she thought he would. She leaned over, grabbed the salt and handed it to him.

Later, after they'd eaten dinner, and Jess had admitted it *was* the best lasagna she'd ever eaten, they were sitting on the couch watching a football game on the television. Jess wasn't really paying attention, but she didn't want to be rude and tell Kason she hated the game. She was going over in her head all that had happened and what she should do next with her life.

There was a knock at the door and Benny stood up. "Stay."

"What am I, a dog?" Jess mock grumbled, but didn't move as Benny got up to answer the door.

He opened it to see his teammates standing there. "Hey."

"Hey, Benny. Got the stuff," Mozart told him gruffly.

Benny looked at his friends, none of them looked

happy. "What the fuck happened?" he asked softly, not wanting Jess to hear them if something went awry.

"Let us in, Benny," Wolf said seriously.

Benny opened the door and the five men entered and stood around the small space. They all looked at Jessyka, who was now standing by the coffee table. They all noticed she kept the couch between them.

"Hey guys…" she began, but stopped when no one returned her greeting.

Benny came over to her and put his hand around her upper arm gently and led her over to the men. "Before you guys say what you need to, let me formally introduce you. I know you know Jess, hell, we've seen her almost every time we've eaten at *Aces*, but everyone, this is Jessyka, with a y-k-a, Allen. Jess, this is Wolf, Abe, Mozart, Cookie, and you already met Dude."

Jess looked at the men. They were certainly good looking, and big, and right now having all their attention on her was a bit unnerving. She was used to them being with their women and not really paying any attention to her. "Hi," was all she could squeak out. She looked back to Kason.

"Did that asshole do all that to you?" Cookie growled.

"Here we go again," Jess said under her breath. She'd made it through Dude's inspection earlier, she wasn't feeling up to another, or four, others.

"Yes, Brian hit me. He hurt me. I'm okay. I have bruises, but they're healing. I'm here, I'm not there anymore. I don't limp because of him. I was born with one leg shorter than the other. I just had the best fucking lasagna I've ever eaten and am feeling fairly mellow after a long, shitty day. Can we please move on?"

Surprisingly, she watched the men's mouths quirk as if they wanted to laugh, but they didn't.

"Yeah, sweets, we can move on," Mozart said for the group.

"Thank God," Jess commented, barely resisting the urge to roll her eyes.

"So we went by today to get your stuff," Wolf said grimly. "There was a lot of shit sitting out by the dumpster, we had a bad feeling about it and when we checked it out, figured it was yours."

Jess gasped. Brian had thrown her stuff away?

Wolf continued. "We loaded it all up to bring to you, and Dude and Abe went to 'speak' with Brian."

"I take it the talk didn't go well," Jessyka said, figuring Brian probably tried to act all macho with the men standing in front of her. He never did know when to keep his mouth shut and when it was appropriate to voice his displeasure.

"Yeah, it didn't go well," Abe responded dryly.

"What'd he do?"

"For starters he copped an attitude with us, which wasn't smart. Then he insulted you, his sister, and someone named Tabitha."

Jess drew in a breath, just hearing Tabitha's name brought back the intense pain she'd felt earlier that day. She'd been able to bank it during dinner and while sitting with Kason, but simply hearing her name brought it all back in an instant.

Kason put his hand on her lower back and slowly massaged her there. His touch pushed the feelings back just enough so she could focus again.

Abe continued, not commenting on her indrawn breath, "We were going to just take a look around and get out of his hair until he started with the threats."

The air in the room turned electric. Jess didn't know how else to describe it. The men were pissed. They were pissed then and they were obviously still pissed now. "Threats?"

"Yeah, telling us he'd fuck you up worse the next time he saw you wasn't his best choice of words. Dude convinced him of the error of his way of thinking," Abe said.

"What did you do?" Jess whispered, horrified, looking at Dude.

"Don't worry about it, Jess," Wolf told her confidently. "Brian won't touch you again."

Jess was horrified. "But you guys could get in trouble. I don't understand why you'd risk your career for me. I know around here all it'll take is one person complaining about something you did and taking it back to the base. Your military career could be hurt because of me."

Dude walked up to Jess, as he had that morning, and put his finger under her chin again. Jess knew she should probably be more freaked out than she was, but as she'd told Kason earlier that night, she knew these guys wouldn't hurt her. But it was obvious they liked to make sure whoever they were talking to, *saw* them while they were talking. Kason's hand on her back went a long way to making her feel safe and comfortable though.

"He won't touch you again," Dude repeated what Wolf had just said. "But, if you see him, turn and walk the other way. Don't engage him. You let one of us know and we'll deal with it."

He wasn't asking. He was telling.

Jess pulled her face out of Dude's grip and looked at the men. "I don't understand any of this, but fine. I don't want anything to do with him ever again, so it's no problem for me to walk away from him."

"We looked around your old place and gathered what we thought was yours," Cookie told her. "Unfortunately, it looked like he'd already removed most of it. What we did find by the dumpster was either broken or destroyed. We found a few bags of your clothes though.

But don't worry, Fiona and the other women are already on a mission to replace every piece of clothing that might have been destroyed... plus enough clothes for you to wear one outfit a day for the next year and not have to repeat anything."

The other men chuckled, obviously knowing their women and their shopping habits.

"But I can't pay them back," Jess fretted, turning to Kason.

"You don't need to pay them back, Jess," Benny reassured her.

"But..."

Wolf interrupted Jessyka before she could protest further. "Jess, this is what friends do. We know you, we like you. You were in a hell of a situation. Any one of us should've done something sooner, but we didn't."

"I don't understand."

"We saw you all the time, Jess. I'm sure Benny has explained this to you. We saw how you were changing in front of our eyes, week after week. We didn't know for sure what Brian was doing to you, but we had our suspicions, but none of us *did* anything. That's on us. This is our way of making it right. And I'd just like to see you *try* to tell Ice or the other women you won't take the things they get for you. If you think we're bad, you haven't seen anything yet."

The men all laughed. Jess didn't know what to say.

Dude hadn't moved, but now leaned down and kissed Jess on the cheek. "I advise you to just go with it, Jess. You won't win." He chucked her under the chin and backed away. "I'll go and get what we brought."

Wolf came up to Jessyka next and kissed the other cheek. "Hang in there, sweetie. Things will get better quickly. Promise."

The other three men came up in sequence and kissed her as well. They all added their support and left to make sure all her things were brought inside.

Jess looked up at Benny. "Your friends are all so nice."

"They're *your* friends now too, Jess."

She blinked. She supposed they were. Jess didn't know how she'd gotten so lucky, but she silently threw a prayer toward the sky. Maybe Tabitha was watching out for her and making sure she was all right. Jess closed her eyes and smiled a small smile.

Chapter Eight

"COME ON, JESS! You have to try that on!" Summer's voice rang through the store.

Jess shook her head. "Summer, I've tried practically everything in the store on already. I'm tired, I'm broke, and I'm ready to go home!"

"Just one more store, you have to see the new stuff they got in!"

Jess sighed and followed Summer out of the store. Kason's teammates' women were awesome. They were funny and down to earth and Jess liked them from the moment they met up that day. She figured she would, since she'd seen them in the bar every week. They never snapped their fingers at her, they were always polite, and they were all great tippers.

She pulled out her phone to text Kason. She'd gotten used to texting him whenever a funny thought struck her. He always responded, sometimes not right away, but at least within a few hours.

Summer is drvig me crazy! Save me!

His response was almost immediate this time.

Too much shopping?

Y!

Kason didn't text back, but Jess wasn't worried. He'd never failed to come through for her. The last month had been unreal for Jessyka. She'd been nervous about living with Kason, but shouldn't have been. He'd set up his extra room for her, provided her with a little TV of her own, so when she needed her own space, she'd have a place to go. He'd given her five hundred dollars so she could buy what she needed. Jess had insisted it be a loan, and Kason had agreed, but she had a feeling she'd have a fight on her hands if she actually tried to pay him back.

So Jess made sure she earned her keep around the apartment. When she did her laundry, she threw his in too. She vacuumed and cleaned the dishes when he cooked.

She quickly learned he was anal about his kitchen and about cooking. Caroline had looked at her like she was an alien from another planet when Jess had told her that she and Kason frequently made dinner together. Caroline explained that Kason never let *anyone* help him. Ever. Even his teammates. The kitchen was his domain and was off limits to anyone when he was cooking.

Jess had been shocked, Kason had never said any-thing to her about it. She'd confronted him about it one night and all he'd said was, "I don't mind when *you* help me."

Jess had let it go because honestly, it was one of her favorite times, when they stood side-by-side in the small kitchen preparing dinner.

When Kason had to work late, Jess always made sure she had something waiting for him when he got home. Jess knew she wasn't as good of a cook as he was, but Kason never made her feel as if what she'd made was any less delicious than what he'd make for himself.

He admitted that most of the time when he lived by himself he just threw a pre-packaged meal in the microwave and ate that for dinner. Jess had been appalled, but Kason just laughed.

Jessyka admitted to herself that she was at a point where she wished for more with Kason, but she honestly had no idea what he thought about her. He touched her all the time. He'd kiss her on the head, he'd put his hand on her waist or the small of her back to steer her around furniture or to where he wanted her to go. When they watched TV, he'd put his arm around her and she'd snuggle into his side, but Jess hadn't seen any signs from him that he wanted anything more than friendship.

Kason hadn't held her in his arms since that first

night. Every now and then when Jess would have a nightmare she craved the feel of Kason's arms around her, to make her feel safe, but she'd lay in her bed, wide-awake, by herself, waiting for her terror to fade.

Living with Kason made her appreciate what he and his teammates went through to stay as in shape as they were. They worked out, or did PT, almost every morning. They would run ten miles along the beach, swim, bike, lift weights... not to mention the mock situations they participated in on the base to keep up to date in extraction techniques or whatever. They were always having meetings and other things they couldn't talk about.

They were very busy men, but every time Jess had called or texted Kason, he'd responded. Jess had no idea how he did it, but it made her feel very special. She'd never felt that way before. Brian had certainly never come running when she lowered herself to ask for his help. She remembered one night when they'd actually been dating, she'd called to let him know she had a flat tire and was nervous since it was late and dark and he'd reprimanded her for calling him because he had to get up early and work. Jess had ended up calling the auto club and it had taken over an hour to get the tire changed before she finally was able to get home. She'd quickly learned not to bother asking for any help from Brian again.

Jessyka had no idea how to find out if Kason actually liked her as more than a friend. She was scared to rock the boat. What if he didn't? She would feel so awkward around him and it would probably ruin their friendship. She felt like she was in junior high and was obsessing over a crush. Jess knew the first step to trying to move their relationship to the next level was to move out of his apartment. She needed to get a place of her own, then maybe she could dip her toe in the waters and see if maybe, if she was lucky, Kason might want to take their relationship past friendship.

Jess startled when Summer's phone rang. They were powerwalking down the mall toward the big department store at the other end.

"Hey, Mozart. *Pause.* I'm shopping with Jessyka. *Pause.* Really? *Pause.* But... *Pause.* Okay, see you soon. *Pause.* Love you too. Bye."

Jess held back the smile that threatened to erupt.

"Oh, Jess, I'm sorry, but that was Mozart. I have to go."

"Is everything all right?"

Jess couldn't help the grin that came over her face when Summer blushed. "Yeah, he got the rest of the afternoon off... he wants me to come home."

"No problem, Summer. We can shop later."

"Yeah."

Jess pulled out her phone as Summer led the way

back through the mall toward the exit that would take them to her car. She shot off a quick text.

Thnk u. U're a lifesvr.

Anything for you gorgeous.

"Summer, can you drop me off at *Aces*? Since I have some extra time I need to stop by and pick up my schedule for the next two weeks. I also want to talk to my boss and see if I can't get some extra hours scheduled."

"Everything okay? Do you need money?"

"You guys are always offering me money," Jess mock grumbled. "No, I'm fine. I've just been thinking about getting out of Kason's hair and moving into my own place. I've just about got enough saved, but if I can get a few more hours I think I can have what I need to be comfortable in another couple of weeks."

Summer got a weird look on her face and looked at Jess as they walked. "Have you spoken to Kason about this yet?"

"Well, no, but I'm planning on it."

"I think you should do that before you make any plans or sign any leases."

"Of course I will, Summer. I'd never disrespect him like that. He's been too much of a good friend to me."

Summer continued to look at her weirdly.

"What? Why are you looking at me like that?"

"What do you think of Kason?"

"Why are you asking me that? You know I like him."

"Yeah, but do you *like* him, or only like him?"

"Are we in junior high school now?" Jess voiced the thought she'd had earlier.

"Just answer the question, Jess." When Jessyka was silent, Summer stopped walking and turned toward her friend. "Look, Caroline is the one who usually does this, but it looks like I have to since you brought it up. Jess, Kason likes you."

"Yeah, I'm his friend, I like him too."

"No, quit acting coy. He *likes* you. Jesus, Jess, do you think he'd let any ol' woman live in his apartment with him? The man is private. He is closed off. Don't take this the wrong way, but he used to have one-night stands all the time. He's never let anyone cook with him before. No. One. But here you are. Living with him. Sharing cooking duties. Texting him to save you from evil girlfriends who want to shop with you." Summer smiled at her last words to take the sting out of them.

Jess blushed, embarrassed Summer knew she'd texted Kason to get her out of the shopping trip.

"What I'm trying to say, is that he wants to be more than friends with you. We don't know what he's waiting for, but I expect it's for you to show him some sign you want that too. If you don't, by all means, move out.

Find your own place. Move on. But if you *like* him, let him know. I guarantee he won't leave you hanging."

"What if it ruins our friendship?"

"Oh, Jess. It won't. I swear. Out of all of us women, you and Kason have known each other the longest before you got together… that is *if* you get together. For most of us it was an instant attraction. While we fought it for a while, it was still quick. But you guys have known each other for *forever* compared to the rest of us. Yes, you're just now really getting to know each other, but you have a base that none of us had because you've lived together as friends. And that's a good thing. All I ask is that you treat him with care. We love Kason. Think about it, will you?"

Jess could only nod. Did Kason really like her more than a friend? She tried to think back through the last month. She tried to analyze their encounters, his touches… Summer interrupted her thoughts.

"Stop thinking so much about it, Jess. Just go with it. Tell him you want to talk to him tonight and let him know how you feel, that you want to know if he has any desire to take your friendship to the next level. If he doesn't, he'll tell you. You can proceed with your plans to get your own place and that will be that. But if he does want to move things along, you'll never find another man more willing and eager to please you and keep you safe, than a Navy SEAL. I can promise you that."

"It scares the crap out of me, but you're right, Summer. Thank you."

"You're welcome." Summer took Jess's arm in hers and pulled her to the exit. "Now text him and let him know I'm dropping you off at the bar and to come and get you in about an hour."

"You're as bossy as your man... did you know that?"

"Yeah, I learned from the best. Now, come on, let's get out of here. I expect you to call or text me the minute you come up for air."

"You're that sure of what Kason's answer will be?"

"Oh yeah. You have no idea what's coming." Summer smiled a secret smile as she pulled Jess to her car. She couldn't wait to get a hold of the other girls and tell them their plan had been set in motion. Hopefully the next time they saw Jess, she'd be one of them for real.

Chapter Nine

I'm rdy whenvr u r 4 u 2 pk me up at bar

I'll be there in twenty minutes. Stay inside until I get there.

Jessyka rolled her eyes at Kason's text. She always acted annoyed at his commands, but deep down, didn't mind. It meant he cared about her. Brian had always been annoyed when she'd asked him to pick her up anywhere, so it was a nice change. She hated to constantly compare Kason to Brian, but the differences were so acute, she couldn't help it.

Jess put the phone down and put her elbows back on the bar. It was mid-afternoon, past the lunch crowd, but before the dinner and bar rush. She'd spoken to her boss and he'd been more than willing to add on some hours for her.

Jess supposed most people would hate working as a waitress, but she honestly enjoyed it. Every day was different and she was good at it. She didn't need to write down orders, she could make change in her head, and she'd excelled over the years at being the type of waitress each group or person wanted. Sometimes she was their friend, other times she kept her interactions to a minimum and more business-like. She even knew how far to take the flirting so it wouldn't be interpreted as a come on.

Jess was lost in her own thoughts about what she was going to say to Kason that night when Brian and a bunch of other men walked in. She hadn't seen him since the night he beat the crap out of her and Tabitha had died. Brian's eyes locked on hers right away. The look he gave her made Jess's heart stop for a moment. Brian had a cast on his arm that went from his fingertips all the way up to his shoulder.

Feeling sick and frightened, even though they were in a public place and there were people all around, Jess grabbed her phone and went into the back of the bar and to the office. She knocked on the door and her boss answered.

"Can I wait in here for Kason to pick me up?"

"Of course, babe. Anything wrong?" Mr. Davis was a big man. He'd been in the Navy for a few years, Jess had no idea how long, but after he'd gotten out he'd bought the bar and had been running it ever since. He'd told her several times how he was thinking about retiring, but Jess would believe it when she saw it. He loved *Aces*. It was his baby.

"My ex just came in. That's all."

Her boss stood up, ready to rush out into the bar area. Kason had sat down with him and had a talk with the bar owner. He wanted to make sure he knew that Brian was dangerous and to keep him away from Jessyka if at all possible. He'd agreed immediately. Mr. Davis might be a retired Navy sailor, and not a SEAL, but he still looked able to defend Jess from anyone who might want to hurt her.

Jess put out her hand toward Mr. Davis, trying to reassure him and make sure he didn't rush out into the bar and kick Brian out. "No, it's okay. He didn't do anything, he just makes me nervous. If I can just wait in here, I'm sure it'll be fine."

"No problem. I know you have those SEAL friends now, but know if you need anything, I'm here for you."

"Thanks, Mr. Davis. I appreciate it. Seriously."

Jess waited in the office, playing solitaire on her phone, until it vibrated.

Here

Jessyka stood up and put her purse over her shoulder. "Thanks, Mr. Davis. Kason's here. I'll see you tomorrow. Thanks again for the extra hours."

"I'll walk you out. And of course you can have the extra hours, Jess. Why you'd doubt I've give them to you is beyond me. You're the best server I've ever had."

Jess shook her head at the man and smiled. She wasn't sure that was true, but it was nice of him to say.

She headed back into the bar next to her boss, nervously looking around for Brian. He was sitting at the other end of the large room, on the other side of what constituted the dance floor at night, glaring at her. His eyes turned into slits and he mouthed something at her. Jess didn't stick around to try to figure out what it was. She walked as fast as she could, without looking desperate, to the door of the bar.

They got to the door and Mr. Davis opened it for her. Jess was relieved to see Kason standing at the passenger side of his car, not too far from the exit. Jess waved at her boss and limped over to Kason as fast as her legs would carry her and hugged him tightly when she reached his side. Her only thought was to feel his arms around her... to feel safe.

"Hey. What's wrong?"

"Nothing, can we just go?"

Benny pulled back from Jess and held her by her upper arms and looked into her eyes. He looked back at her boss, standing in the doorway of the bar then back to Jess. Something was definitely wrong, but a parking lot out in the open wasn't the place to discuss it. She looked okay otherwise, no visible injuries and that made Benny feel better.

"Okay, Jess, we're going. Hop in."

Jess didn't waste any time and climbed into the safety of his car. Kason closed her door and she watched as he stalked around the hood and got into the driver's seat. He put the car in drive and headed out without a word.

Jessyka couldn't resist, and turned her head around to look back at the bar as they pulled away. The door was now shut and no one came out, no one followed after her. She breathed a sigh of relief and turned back to the front windshield.

It wasn't until Kason spoke that Jess realized she probably should've been a bit more circumspect in her actions.

"I don't know what the hell you're looking for, but you better be ready to talk to me when we get home."

Jess looked over and saw a muscle ticking in Kason's jaw. His hands were flexing on the steering wheel and his body was tight. Uh oh.

"I'm okay, Kason. Nothing happened."

"But something freaked you out."

Shit. He was too smart for his own good. "Yeah." Jess put her hand on Kason's thigh and felt it jump under her touch before relaxing a fraction.

No more words were spoken as Kason drove them back to the apartment. He parked and came around the car and helped Jess out. He put his hand on the small of her back and followed her to the door. He unlocked the locks and guided her in. Once inside, Kason threw his keys into the basket by the door and crossed his arms over his chest.

"We're home. Spill."

Jess didn't hesitate. She put her purse on the table next to the bowl of keys and turned to Kason. "Brian came into the bar while I was waiting for you."

"Fuck."

"It's okay, he didn't talk to me at all."

"Then why are you all jacked up, Jess?"

"It sounds stupid."

Benny took a step forward and pulled Jess into his arms. He put one hand behind her head and pressed it into his chest. The other he wrapped around her waist until they were touching from their hips up to her head. "It's not stupid." His voice eased a bit.

"He looked at me funny."

Instead of laughing at her, Benny simply asked, "In what way?"

Jess took a deep breath, inhaling the scent of Kason. She'd never grow tired of it. He smelled like the soap he used that morning and… man. She had no idea how to describe it. It was probably a mixture of his sweat and his natural scent, but it was an immediate aphrodisiac to her. Jess could feel her nipples tighten. It was completely inappropriate, but she couldn't help it. Remembering he'd asked her a question, she finally answered him.

"He was pissed. He came in with a group of men and he looked right at me and glared. I went into the back to Mr. Davis's office to wait for you. When you got there and I went to leave, he squinted his eyes at me and mouthed something. I don't know what it was because I hightailed it out of there."

"Good girl," Benny soothed. "You did good."

Without looking up, Jess told him, whispering, "He had a cast on his arm."

"Yeah, I know."

At that, Jess did look up. "You know?"

"Yeah, the guys did that to him when they went to get your stuff."

Jess could only stare at Kason in surprise and dismay. She could only parrot his words back to him. "The guys did that?"

"Yeah. I told you he was being an ass. They had to convince him they were serious. He now knows if he fucks with you again, they'll fuck with *him* again. Simple."

Jess put her head back on Kason's chest and tried to work out in her mind what she thought about what his friends had done.

"You need to talk this through?"

"Maybe."

"Okay, let me make us something to eat. You go take a hot bath, try to relax. It'll be ready in about an hour. That enough time?"

Jess nodded, but didn't move out of Kason's arms.

Benny loved the feel of Jessyka in his arms. He wanted nothing more than to carry her into his room and strip off all her clothes and make her relax the best way he knew how, but he had to know she wanted it first. He pulled back and put his hand on her cheek.

"An hour?"

"Yeah, okay, Kason."

Benny couldn't resist and he leaned to her and kissed her forehead. Then her nose, then for the first time since she'd moved in with him, he touched his lips to hers. He kept the contact light and unthreatening. "Go run your bath, gorgeous."

Benny watched as Jess licked her lips, as if tasting him all over again. "Okay," she whispered before stepping away from him.

Jess turned and limped away and Benny repressed the groan that threatened to come out of his throat. He wasn't kidding when he'd told her a month or so ago that her gait was sexy as hell. Her hips swayed seductively back and forth as she walked. It was more of a turn on to watch her walk than any practiced runway model he'd ever seen. Part of the allure was that she had absolutely no idea how sexy she was. None. No idea at all. Totally clueless.

Benny turned to the kitchen. He had an hour to

whip up some comfort food for his woman. He knew Jess had some heavy thoughts running around in her head, but Benny hoped after they talked she'd be okay with what was happening.

Fifty minutes later, Jess wandered out of the back hall. She was wearing the same T-shirt she'd borrowed the first day she'd been there. Benny smiled. She'd refused to give it back, claiming he'd given it to her and she wasn't giving it back. Benny had no problem with that at all. She could steal any shirt of his she wanted. He loved seeing her in his clothes, and could imagine what she wasn't wearing underneath it.

Her hair was wet. It wasn't quite long enough to go back in a scrunchie, but it was getting there. Jess had explained how she'd cut her hair because Brian had liked to yank on it to get her attention. Kason had held back the harsh words he wanted to say and had simply told her he liked her hair short or long, as long as she was happy with it.

Jess was flushed from the heat of the bath and Benny could see a sheen of sweat on her brow. She was gorgeous and Benny knew he'd never wanted a woman as badly as he wanted this one.

"Go sit on the couch, we'll eat there."

"Can I help?"

"Thank you, no, I got it. Let me spoil you."

"You're always spoiling me."

"Yeah, so let me keep doing it. Sit." Benny smiled as he said it so Jess would know he was teasing. He relaxed as she smiled back and went to do as he'd asked.

Benny got together the plate with dinner on it as well as napkins. He stuck two water bottles under his arm and headed over to Jess.

"Jesus, Kason, you should've let me help. I could've carried something."

"I said I got it." Benny leaned down and let Jess take the bottles out from under his arm. He turned and put the plate on the coffee table and settled in next to her. He yanked the blanket off the back of the couch and pulled Jess into his side. He put the blanket over her lap, making sure she wouldn't be chilled after her bath.

Then he reached out and grabbed the plate of food and leaned back again, resettling Jess against him.

"What'd you make?"

"Pizza roll ups."

"From scratch?"

"Yeah."

Jess smiled, his words said yes, but his tone said "duh."

Jessyka reached for one of the crescent rolls and Kason held them out of her reach.

"Uh uh. I got this." Benny picked up one of the homemade pizza rolls and blew on it, making sure it wouldn't burn her when she bit into it. He took a bite, and finding the temperature acceptable, held it to Jess.

She looked at him, incredulously.

"Open."

When Jess started to raise her hand to take the roll from his hand, Benny held it up out of her reach. "Open," he repeated.

Jess opened her mouth and didn't take her eyes off of Kason's as he brought the roll down to her mouth. He placed part of it between her teeth and she bit down. Some of the sauce dripped out, but before it could fall, Kason caught it with his finger. He brought his finger up to his mouth and sucked on it, licking away the red sauce he'd just wiped from her mouth.

Neither looked away from each other. Jess finished chewing the first bite and Kason held the rest of the pizza up to her lips. She opened dutifully, and felt Kason's thumb brush against her lip as she closed her lips around the delicious crescent roll.

Kason continued to feed her. He took turns between eating himself, and feeding her. Each time, he took a bite of the roll first, making sure it wasn't too hot, before letting her take a bite.

Jessyka felt weird. She knew she was supposed to be freaking out about Brian and what the SEALs had done to him, but she just didn't have it in her at the moment. Between the bath, being held in Kason's arms, and him feeding her, she was one big marshmallow.

When the pizza rolls were gone, Kason leaned over and placed the now empty plate back on the coffee table. He leaned back to the couch and turned, taking Jess with him.

Benny held on to the woman in his arms as he turned them around on the couch. He moved so he was on his back and Jess's back was to the back of the couch. She was half lying on him and half lying on the couch. Her head rested on his shoulder and one of her arms was lying over his stomach. He had one arm wrapped around her shoulders and the other rested lightly on her hand on his stomach. He sighed in contentment.

Benny hadn't allowed himself the luxury of cuddling with Jess since that first night she'd been in his apartment. Oh, she'd leaned into him on the couch while they watched TV, but it wasn't like this. He wanted to give her space. He didn't want to push her into anything she might not be ready for. But he wanted her. He wanted her more now than he did a month ago. Benny knew all the important things he needed to know about Jess, except for one. How she felt about him.

Benny had spent the last month fantasizing about her. It wasn't enough he woke up hard and had to take care of it before he could go to PT, but every night he went to bed hard, imagining how Jess looked spread out on her bed just one door down from him. He'd had to wash his sheets a lot more often now that Jessyka was living with him.

"Are you comfortable? Your leg doesn't hurt?"

"I'm perfect, Kason. This is perfect."

Benny pulled Jess toward him and kissed her forehead once before settling back again. "Good. Now, talk to me."

Jess didn't hesitate, but laid out what she was thinking. "It's not that I care about Brian, because at this point I don't. But I'm worried about the guys. What if Brian goes to the cops? What if they get in trouble? What if Brian goes after Caroline or any of the others? What if…"

"Shhhh, hang on, gorgeous, let me address your fears one by one, okay?" Benny waited until Jess nodded against him before continuing. "First, Brian won't go to the cops. It's already on file what he did to you. Remember, they took pictures in the hospital. Brian knows it'd be his word against a SEAL's. Who do you think would win in that battle?" Not waiting for her response he went on.

"Wolf talked to our Commander about what happened, essentially giving him a head's up. Of course he didn't give him all the details, but enough that if he heard about it through official channels he could defend the team. And lastly, there's no way in hell Brian would go after the women. He knows he's outmanned and outgunned. Besides, they're all monitored 24/7."

"What do you mean?"

Benny sighed. He had no idea how Jess would take this. He knew he had to give her some background. "How much of the history of the girls do you know?"

Jess looked up at Kason. He sounded so serious. "I know some, but obviously not enough if the look on your face is anything to go by."

Benny put his hand on Jess's head and encouraged her to lay back down. "Wolf met Caroline on a plane that was taken over by hijackers. They survived it, but the bad guys came after her and kidnapped her. Alabama fled from Abe because he did a dumbass thing and hurt her. It was weeks before we could find her. She'd been living on the damn streets. Cookie met Fiona when he was sent into Mexico to rescue another woman that had been taken by white-slavers. She'd been in captivity for about three months when we got her out and no one had even known or cared she was gone. Summer was taken by a man who'd kidnapped, tortured, and murdered Mozart's little sister when he was in high school. Cheyenne had a bomb strapped to her chest...twice. And finally, you know what happened to Cheyenne, Summer, and Fiona when they were taken from the bar not too long ago."

Benny took a deep breath. Now the hard part. "All the guys got together and agreed this shit had to end. We have a friend who lives in Virginia... Tex. He used to be a SEAL, but got hurt and now does some computer shit from out east. He can find anyone. We've literally used him to save the lives of every single one of the guys' women. He does illegal crap we pretend we don't know about, and he knows people in every branch of the military and probably in every state. We overlook anything illegal he might do because it's effective and has saved us more times than not. He monitors the girls. They're tracked all the time. Every day, every move they make."

"But, Kason…"

"I wasn't done. Let me finish then I'll answer whatever questions you have." Benny waited for Jess's agreement, then continued. "They know about it. They agreed to it. They all have issues related to what happened to them. It makes them feel better knowing their men will be able to get to them if, God-forbid, something happens again. The work we do is dangerous. The last thing we want is for some asshole we captured, injured, defeated, whatever, to come back and try to get revenge by taking our women. Their shoes are tracked, their bags, some of their clothes. They even have several pieces of jewelry that have tracking devices in them. Jess, if you remember nothing else, remember this. The women know about it and agreed to it. This is not us being manipulative, controlling assholes, which I admit, we all can be. But this is not that.

"So while Brian doesn't know about any of that, the guys made it clear if he even *thinks* about coming after their women, he'll pay. And how he'll pay would be completely unconnected to us. Tex knows people. I know for a fact he's as close to a team of Delta Force operatives as he is with us. Payment could be arranged without any of us being involved in any way."

"This sounds like the mob or something, Kason. I don't like it."

"I know, and I'm sorry, Jess. But it's how we are. We're a family, yes, sort of like the mob, but we don't go around hurting and intimidating people for the hell of it. In fact, I think this is the only time the guys have taken Tex up on his repeated offers to allow him to be involved."

Benny let his words sink in. The silence stretched out for at least five minutes, but it didn't feel uncomfortable.

At last Jess spoke, "You really think I'm safe? He won't come after me?"

"I really think you're safe. If I didn't think so, I'd tell you. I'd tell you so you could be more vigilant, more aware. I'd never hide that from you."

"Are you tracking me?"

Finally. It was the question Benny had expected from the second he'd mentioned tracking the other women. "No."

"Why not?"

That was *not* what he expected her to say. "I told you the girls know about the devices. I would never do that to you without your consent."

Without looking up, Jess said in a voice that cracked, "I think it'd make me feel safer."

"Then I'll set it up." Benny didn't hesitate in agreeing.

"But Kason, it's different for me. I'm just..." Jess paused thinking about how she wanted to word her thoughts and about what Summer had told her that day. "I'm not *with* you. I'm just your friend. It's not the same."

Benny slid out from under Jessyka and moved her until she was flat on her back on the couch and he was leaning over her. He had one elbow next to her head and his hand curled around the side of her neck.

"How honest can I be with you right now, Jess? I've been pretty forthcoming tonight. Can you take more?"

"From you? Yes."

Benny didn't hesitate or prevaricate. "I want you. Yes, you're my friend, but I want more. I want to be your lover. I want you to sleep in my bed. I want to see you lying on my sheets naked and waiting for me. I want to see you in the shower in the mornings while I'm shaving. You're already doing my laundry and cooking for me when I'm not home to do it for myself. We're already acting like a couple, just without the intimacy. I wanted to give you space. I wanted you to be sure. I've been sure for a while now. I've wanted you in my bed since about a week after you moved in."

"Is that all you want, Kason? Because I don't think I can handle just a sexual relationship with you. I'm too emotionally involved."

"Hell, no, that isn't all I want. If all I wanted was to get off, I could do that any day of the week. I want *you*, Jess. You have no idea how badly I want you, all of you. I want to be free to hold your hand whenever and wherever I want. I want to pull you down in my lap and wrap my arms around you when you come up to me at *Aces*. I want to claim you, to make it so no other guy looks at you while you're walking with your sexy gait. I want everyone to know you're mine. Can you handle that?"

"Yeah, I think I can," Jess smiled at Kason, happier than she'd been in a long time.

They both looked at each other, breathing heavily.

"Did we just agree to 'go together'?"

Benny laughed. "I haven't heard that term since I was in the seventh grade. And no, we didn't agree to 'go together.' You agreed that you're mine. You agreed that I'd take care of you and keep you safe. You agreed to sleep in my bed, shower in my bathroom when I'm in there too, and let me put my hands and lips on you whenever and wherever I want."

"Uh…"

"I'm going to kiss you now, Jess, and I'm not stopping until we're both so exhausted, we're comatose in my bed."

Benny waited for her agreement. He'd never do anything she didn't want him to do.

"God, please, Kason. I've waited forever to really feel your lips on mine."

Benny lowered his head to take what was finally his.

Chapter Ten

BENNY DIDN'T EASE into the kiss, he slammed his lips onto Jessyka's and felt goose bumps form on his arms as she immediately opened for him. Jess wasn't coy, she didn't hesitate, she took all he gave her.

He plunged his tongue inside her mouth and reveled in her taste. Benny had never gotten so turned on by a mere kiss before. If he hadn't waited so long to be inside her, to be right where he was, he could've spent all night simply kissing her. But he was too impatient. He needed to see her, all of her. Benny needed Jess in his territory, on his bed.

He broke the kiss and pushed himself up. Benny could feel his hardness push deeper into the vee of Jess's legs. He smiled and groaned as he felt her hips push up against him.

"You are so fucking sexy, and all mine. Come on, I need to get you in my bed." It didn't seem too fast, they'd gotten to know each other very well over the last month, and it felt right, now that they'd cleared the air, to take the next step.

Benny levered himself up and off the couch and held out a hand to Jess. She didn't hesitate, but immediately put her hand in his and allowed him to pull her up and off the couch, the blanket falling unnoticed by either of them to the floor.

"Walk in front of me, Jess. I want to see your hips sway and know that soon I'll have them all to myself. You have no idea how badly I've wanted to see those hips and that ass on my sheets."

Jess blushed, but did as Kason asked. Feeling bold, she exaggerated her limp as she made her way down the short hallway, smiling as she heard Kason groan. He was fun to tease, especially when she knew her teasing would end with her satisfaction, at least she hoped it would.

She entered his room and inhaled deeply. It smelled like him. She turned around once she entered and faced Kason.

He was ripping his shirt over his head. "Take off your shirt, gorgeous. Let me see you."

Without thinking twice, Jess began to unfasten the buttons on her shirt.

Benny stalked over to her and brushed her hands away from her shirt. "Too slow, lift your arms."

Jess just smiled at the impatience in his voice. Soon Kason's mouth was at her neck. "I saw how you reacted to Dude's words all those weeks ago about marks on a woman's neck. I need to see *my* mark on you. I need everyone else to see it as well."

Jess had never had so much fun during foreplay or sex before. "Well, since we're 'going together,' I suppose it's mandatory to have a hickey too."

She felt Kason's lips curl up into a smile before she groaned and let her head fall back. He sucked hard on her neck and she felt his teeth nip and his tongue soothe over her skin as he did it. His other hand was busy on her breast. Kason hadn't removed her bra yet, but his fingers played over and under the cup, teasing her nipple into hardness.

"Oh God, Kason. Yeah. That feels so good."

Without removing his hand from her breast, his other hand brushed down Jessyka's side. Benny raised his head long enough to murmur in a satisfied voice, "Goosebumps," then he returned to her neck.

He kept his lips on her, but backed them up until her legs hit his mattress. Benny kept pushing until Jess had no choice but to sit. Finally his head came up and he looked into her eyes as both hands went to her breasts. He played and teased there, running his fingers under her bra and over her nipples, before backing away and merely running his hands over the cups themselves.

Jess ran her own hands up and down his body as he caressed hers. Kason's chest was amazing. Hard and cut. He didn't have an ounce of fat anywhere on him, at least not that Jess could see. She couldn't help herself, and brought her fingers up to his nipples and pinched them.

Benny groaned and grabbed Jess's wrists. "Oh no, much more of that and this'll be finished before we even start."

Jess mock-pouted at Kason. "But I want to play too."

"Oh, you'll get to play, don't worry, but it's my turn first. You're lucky enough to be able to get off several times, while we poor men have to settle for one at a time."

"Several times?" Jess asked in bewilderment.

"Oh shit. Really? You don't already know this? Fuck, this is gonna be fun. Take off your bra and lean back."

Jess could only watch as Kason took a step back from her. She immediately felt the loss. Jess quickly put her arms behind her and undid the hook on her bra. She let it fall off her arms and onto the floor and she scooted back on the bed and lay back, as Kason had asked.

"Close your eyes and just feel."

She immediately shut her eyes. Jess knew at this point she'd do just about anything Kason asked of her, and they both knew it.

Jess felt Kason's hands at her waistband. He undid the button of her jeans and she heard the zipper lowering. But instead of pulling them off, he simply ran his fingers around her stomach and the waistband.

"I've spent weeks wondering what you look like here. Do you shave? Are you completely bare? Or do you trim down here so that you only have a small patch? Maybe you don't do anything and you're as wild as your personality. Do I dare guess which one it is, gorgeous?"

When Jess opened her mouth to answer his rhetorical question she felt one of his fingers press over her lips. "No, don't tell me. I want to find out on my own."

Finally Kason tugged off her jeans. She was mostly naked, covered only by her black cotton panties. Jess's breaths came out in pants. She was so ready for this.

"Open your eyes, look at me."

Jess's eyes popped open and met Kason's. "Beautiful. You look beautiful against my sheets, in my bed." His words made her nipples tighten further. His eyes roamed over her body then came up to her eyes.

"Once we do this, I'm not letting you go, Jess. Be sure."

"I'm sure." Her words were strong and immediate. "If we do this, you're mine too. It goes both ways."

"Shit yeah, it does. I'm yours, you're mine. Fuck, I love that."

Jess smiled. Kason's language got dirtier and dirtier the more turned on he got.

Prolonging the anticipation of knowing what she

looked like under her panties, Benny leaned down and tasted her nipple for the first time. Jess wasn't overly endowed, but what she had was perfect. Benny didn't know sizes, but she fit in the palm of his hands perfectly. He squeezed her breasts and then brought his index fingers and thumbs to her nipples. "You like to tease, Jess?"

Jessyka arched her back. God, his fingers felt so good. She moved restlessly under him. "Jesus, Kason, please!"

"Please what, gorgeous?"

"I don't know!" Jess looked up to see the broad smile on Kason's face.

"Oh yeah, this is gonna be fun."

He lifted his hands off of her and leaned back on his knees above her. Benny's hands went to the waistband of his own jeans and he torturously eased his zipper down. As soon as the zipper got below a certain point, the head of his cock poked through the hole in his boxers.

Jess couldn't help but giggle.

Benny smiled. He'd never laughed during sex before. Everything felt new with Jess.

"He looks excited to come out and play."

"Oh, he's excited all right, but he'll just have to wait. I have stuff I gotta do first."

"Stuff?"

"Stuff," he confirmed with a smile.

Jess watched as Kason leaned to the side and shucked his jeans one leg at a time. He then scooted down on the bed until his face was right over her now damp panties. He drew his index finger down over the seam, then back up.

"Soaked."

Jess moaned. "Yeah… please."

"For me."

"Yeah, Kason. For you."

"I like."

Jess didn't answer him that time, knowing he was playing with her. Instead she bent her knees and spread her legs.

"Oh yeah, I can smell how much you want me. You do want this, right, Jess?"

"Duh, Kason. Yeah. Can you please get on with it? 'Cos I'm dying here."

Apparently her words pushed Kason over the edge because he reached to the bedside table and grabbed a knife. He flicked it open and looked up at Jess.

She didn't even flinch, just raised her hips and murmured, "Oh, fuck yeah."

Benny smiled. "You aren't worried what I'm gonna do with this?"

"You'd better be cutting my panties off and going down on me if you know what's good for you."

Benny laughed. Jess was fucking perfect. This was a side of her he'd sensed was lurking below her beaten-down persona. Brian had bent her, but hadn't broken her. "Don't move." He placed one hand on her stomach and pressed down, making sure she wouldn't inadvertently twitch or move. Benny didn't want to cut her, just the elastic on the underwear she was sporting. He put the blade under one side of the cloth at her hip and tugged upward. It didn't take much pressure, Benny, as did every good SEAL, kept his blade razor sharp. He then moved to her other hip and did the same thing. He flicked the blade shut and threw it toward the nightstand. It clattered to a stop, resting against the wall.

Knowing nothing would stop him now, Benny slowly peeled down the front of Jess's panties and sighed in appreciation. She wasn't bare, but was well trimmed. She'd shaved the lips of her sex, but left a nice sized patch of hair above. He ran his fingers over it. "Fuck woman," he breathed, then lowered his head.

Jessyka had been nervous about what he'd think of her grooming choice, but soon forgot everything, including her own name. Kason had been right, females certainly *could* go more than once, as long as they had a man who knew what he was doing.

And Kason *definitely* knew what he was doing. It wasn't until she'd begged him to stop, that he'd sat up and wiped his hand over his mouth. "God, you taste good. I swear, Jess, I could do that all night."

Jessyka smiled weakly up at him. She'd only had one lover before Kason, and Brian certainly didn't compare at all. "Your turn, Kason."

"No, now it's *our* turn."

Kason slid off the bed and stood up so he could remove his boxers. His cock was hard and straining upward. It certainly didn't look comfortable to Jessyka. He opened the drawer next to the bed and pulled out a brand new box of condoms. He quickly opened the box and grabbed one and put it on. He crawled back on the bed and over to Jess.

"Are you ready for me?"

"I think I've been ready for you all my life."

At her words, Jess watched as Kason's face got soft and he leaned down to kiss her. She felt him ease inside her at the same time. He went slowly, somehow understanding how long it'd been for her. When he was all the way in, he sighed and pulled back just enough to see her face.

Jess could see the strain on his face. He was holding back. She hated it. "Let go, Kason. I can take it. I won't break."

"It's been a while for you, gorgeous, I don't want to hurt you."

"You won't hurt me. God, Kason, you prepared me

so well, after two orgasms, I'm soaked. I can take whatever you have. Let go. Make me yours."

"You fucking *are* mine." It was as if his words loosened something inside him. He pulled back and slammed into her. Jess could feel his balls hit up against her body as he bottomed out. She put her arms around him and dug her fingers into his butt.

"Yes, Kason. Again. Do that again."

He did it again, then again. Kason arched his back and his hips pounded into her. Jess leaned up and latched onto his pectoral muscle, right next to his nipple. She sucked in as hard as she could, using her teeth to nibble while she was sucking. If Kason could mark her as his, Jess could do the same right back.

When she was satisfied she'd left a good sized mark, she pulled back and looked up. Kason was smiling down at her, obviously having watched her mark him. "Satisfied?"

"Oh yeah, mine."

"Yours. Fuck, Jess. Yours."

Benny had never felt so connected to another person in his life. He thought the bond he had with his SEAL team was tight, but it was nothing compared to this. Watching her mark his skin was sexy as hell. He wanted to crawl inside Jessyka and never leave. He wanted to imprint her on his skin and imprint himself on hers in return. With that thought, Benny's heart sped up and he couldn't get the image of his release all over her skin out of his mind.

"I want to do something."

"Yes, anything."

Benny smiled. Jess didn't even know what it was that he wanted, but she'd agreed nonetheless.

"I want to paint you with my come. Mark you."

"Yes, Kason, God yes. That's hot as hell."

"Give me one more gorgeous, one more time, then it'll be my turn." Benny leaned up and reached down between their bodies to rub Jess's clit. He continued to pound into her, but rubbed against her bundle of nerves at the same time. Benny felt Jess's inner muscles squeeze and flutter around his dick as she came closer and closer to orgasm.

"That's it, Jess, that's it. Let go. Give it to me."

Jess put her head back and dug her nails into Kason's biceps. "Oh yes. God that feels good. I'm coming…"

Benny could feel the second Jessyka lost it as her inner muscles contracted and gripped him tightly as he continued to push his way in and out of her tight sheath throughout her climax. The second Jess stopped shaking, Benny pulled out and yanked off the condom. There was no way he could hold off his own release any longer. "Look at me, Jess. Watch what you do to me."

Jessyka opened her eyes and looked down. She'd

never seen anything more erotic in all her life. Kason was still straddling her, but he was stroking his cock quickly up and down, aiming at her stomach. She reached for him, wanting to feel his hardness in her hand, but was too late. He threw his head back and erupted. Jess watched, fascinated as Kason continued to spurt in pulses throughout his climax. She brought her hand down to her stomach and smeared his release into her skin, even as he continued emptying himself onto her.

Benny finally opened his eyes after what seemed to be the most intense climax he'd ever had, only to see Jess running both her hands through his release on her stomach. When she saw him watching, she reached down further and caressed his softening cock, squeezing one last stream of fluid from him.

"God, that was sexy as hell," she told him, no artifice in her face or tone. "I loved watching that, and I love feeling you on me."

Benny brought one of his hands up to her face. "Taste me." He couldn't stop the order if he tried. But Jess, being Jess, didn't hesitate. She brought one of her hands up to his wrist and guided his thumb into her mouth. Benny could feel his own wetness from her hand as she held his wrist. She licked and sucked all of his release off his finger, then nipped the pad of his thumb as she let go.

Benny let himself drop down gently on top of her. He could feel the wetness between her legs as she drew one leg up and over his hip. He could feel his own release between them on her stomach just as he could feel her wet hand run over his back and down to his ass.

He chuckled. "We need a shower."

"I like us like this. It's real. Raw. I've never had it this way. It was always polite and neat."

"I don't want to hear anything about how it used to be again," Benny warned, not lifting his head.

"I only meant that this means something to me. I like it. I like us. Some people might think this is gross, but I think it's natural and real. Can we just stay here for a bit?"

"Of course. But don't blame me when you're sticky and uncomfortable."

Jess laughed. "Okay. I won't. Promise."

Later that night, much later, after a shower which included both of them climaxing again, Benny thought about how he'd gotten to this point in his life. He was happy for the first time ever. Genuinely happy. He might not know how he'd gotten there, but he knew he never wanted it to change.

Chapter Eleven

JESSYKA LOOKED OVER at Fiona as they pulled up to Caroline and Wolf's house. She wasn't sure about this. While she liked all of the women, a slumber party was a bit beyond what she was used to.

"Maybe you should take me back home, Fiona."

"No way. This is tradition. Every time the guys get sent off on a mission we all get together and get drunk and cry and worry about them, then we get on with life until they get home. You're one of us now, so you belong here with us."

The whole "being one of them now" was still so unreal to Jessyka. It hadn't taken long for the guys, and their women, to figure out her and Kason's relationship had changed. Hell, the guys had taken one look at the hickey on Kason's chest the first time they'd had PT and known. The same with the girls when they'd seen the not-so-subtle mark Kason had left on her neck.

Jess blushed, but Summer had just given her a huge hug and said, "Told you so."

A week after Jess and Kason had solidified their new relationship, the team had been called on a mission. They couldn't say where they were going or when they'd be back. That was the hardest part about being with a SEAL. They'd get called off on the spur of the moment and couldn't say anything about where they were going or when they might return.

Jess had cried a bit, but Kason just held her tight and told her to trust him. That he knew what he was doing and so did the team. They'd be back as soon as they could.

So here she was, packed for a slumber party of all things. Mr. Davis had given her the night off from *Aces* and she was apparently stuck until she could escape in the morning.

"Hey you guys! It's about time you got here!" Caroline was standing at the front door waving frantically at them.

"Looks like they started without us," Fiona said laughing as she got their bags out of the trunk of the car.

And they *had* gotten started without them. Once they'd gotten inside it was obvious Caroline and Alabama were already three sheets to the wind and Summer and Cheyenne weren't too far behind them.

"We're so glad you're here, Jess! Seriously! We just *knew* Kason would find someone soon, we just had no idea it would be *you*! You're awesome!"

Jess could just smile at her.

"Here! You have to catch up! Try this! We just invented it tonight!" Alabama thrust a glass filled with what looked like milk in it. "I know it looks gross, but try it anyway!"

Jessyka took a small sip, dreading what it would taste like, and looked up in surprise.

"Ha! Told you it was good! Tastes like the milk left over after you've eaten a bowl of cinnamon cereal doesn't it?"

"Oh my God! That's *exactly* what it tastes like! What is it?" Jess couldn't believe how good the drink tasted. She wasn't one for the taste of hard alcohol, but she couldn't really taste anything in this.

"It's Rum Chata and vanilla cake vodka."

"Rum what?"

"Don't ask, just drink!"

And they did. Eventually they moved their party to the basement and lay sprawled on the bed, floor, and a fluffy chair in the corner of the room.

The room was slowly spinning around Jessyka, but she felt like she was floating, so it was okay.

"I don't like it when the guys are gone," Cheyenne said in a lull in the conversation.

"We don't either, but we have each other, and it gets easier," Caroline said confidently.

"How can it get easier? They're out there getting

shot at or something worse," Cheyenne grumbled.

"Because they're good at what they do. Because they'll come home. Because we're tough as nails Navy SEAL women and we have to deal with it," was Alabama's answer.

Asking what she never would've asked if she hadn't been drinking for the last three hours, Jess piped up. "Aren't you nervous without them around? I mean scared for yourself?"

Not beating around the bush, Fiona asked for clarification. "You mean like someone's gonna kidnap us again?"

"Well, yeah. Or hurt you, or rob you, or something."

"No. We have Tex," Fiona said matter-of-factly.

"Tex. Kason said something about Tex," Jess said absently.

"You mean he hasn't programmed your phone with his number yet?" Summer asked in bewilderment.

"No, I don't think so," Jess said honestly.

Fiona didn't say anything else, just pulled her cell phone out of her pocket and hit some buttons. Soon they all heard through the speaker, the ringing of a phone.

"Hey, Fiona, what's up?"

"Tex!"

"Yeah girl, you called me. What do you need?"

"Kason hasn't programmed your number into Jess's phone yet," Fiona said, as if this was a federal offense.

"Yeah, well, he hasn't set up tracers yet either," Tex replied calmly.

"Are you kidding?"

All eyes in the room turned to Jess. She looked at all the women looking at her and threw both her hands up as if to say, "don't look at me."

"This is not acceptable at all!" Fiona exclaimed to no one. Remembering Tex was on the line she leaned down and said too loudly into the speaker, "Tex!"

"How much have y'all had to drink tonight?"

"Whatever, listen, Tex. You have to get some thingies on Jess!"

"I will, once Benny tells me he's talked to her about it."

Jess thought it was about time she broke in and prevented world war three. "I know about the tracking thingies. Kason told me about them."

Five sets of eyes swiveled to her and Jess swallowed hard.

"And?" Cheyenne demanded.

"And what?" Jess prevaricated, not knowing exactly what it was she was supposed to say.

"Are you gonna be all high and mighty and disapprove or what?" Alabama's tone was a bit belligerent and Jess immediately got defensive.

Forgetting Tex was still listening, Jess let the women know exactly what she was thinking. "I don't disapprove. Shit, knowing what you guys all went through, I'm amazed you're still upright and functioning normally in society. If I'd been through what you had, I'd probably be in a fetal position on the floor crying and moaning and not wanting to see anybody ever again. I figure part of the reason why you're so awesome is because of your men. So you know what, if I was you, I'd want to have a GPS surgically implanted under my skin, like a microchip that dogs get. To know that you have a man who'd do anything to protect you, to go so far as to want to know where you are every minute of every day just so he knows you're safe? Hell yeah, I want that. But I'm not you. I haven't been stolen out of my bed at night. I haven't been kidnapped by scary people wanting to do scary things. I'm just me. And besides, Kason hasn't asked me. He told me about you guys, but he hasn't told me he wants to put a tracking thingie on me. So there."

It was a lame finish to her impassioned speech, but Jess wound down quickly after blurting out the truth. The truth that she hadn't been able to get off her mind since Kason had told her about how all the other women were tracked. He hadn't brought it up again and she didn't know if it was because he didn't want her like that, or because he thought she'd disapprove or what.

"Jessyka, go upstairs and get your purse."

Jess turned to look at the phone in confusion. "Huh?"

"Go upstairs and get your purse. Bring it back down to the basement. We'll wait for you," Tex repeated, as if talking to a child.

"I'll get it!" Cheyenne yelled, leaping up and stumbling up the stairs as if she was an eight year old and not thirty two.

They heard Cheyenne clomping back down the stairs not fifteen seconds later. "Got it!" she yelled, almost tripping and landing on her face as she got to the last step.

"Jessyka, open it up and look in the side pocket," Tex's voice was calm, but at the same time it was obvious he wasn't asking, he was telling.

Jess did as Tex asked and pulled out a small black square. It was about the size of her thumbnail. "What the hell is this?"

"It's a tracking thingie!" Fiona cried happily.

"But, Tex, you said that you hadn't…"

"I said *I* hadn't. I didn't say Benny hadn't already taken care of it."

The room was quiet for a moment, everyone taking in what had just happened.

"Kason put this in my purse?" Jess whispered looking down at the innocent looking small black device in her hand incredulously. "But I thought he didn't…"

"No, he wanted to," Tex interrupted Jessyka before she could continue. "He called me about a week ago and said he wanted me to track you the same way I tracked everyone else. I refused."

"Tex!" Summer admonished. "That's mean!"

"Let me finish, darlin'. I refused because he hadn't gotten your permission yet. I won't ever track any of you women without you approving it. Benny was planning on talking to you about it, but then they got called away. He was in a panic because he hadn't been able to talk to you yet and he didn't want to rush it, but he also didn't want to go on a mission and leave you vulnerable. I agreed to one tracking device in your purse. I've got all the others waiting to be set up for when he gets back home."

"Why did he panic?" Jess asked, her words slurring a bit. She was obviously more drunk than she thought.

"Because every damn time they go on a mission it seems like one of you girls gets in trouble. So in order to prevent that from happening this time to you, Jess, he wanted you tracked before he left. Are you guys going to get in trouble this time? I swear to God, every time they leave I'm stuck to my chair making sure nothing goes wrong with you ladies."

"Nothing's going to go wrong!" Caroline told him with authority. Of course her statement would've been a bit more believable if she hadn't hiccupped in the middle of it.

"Right. Okay, if ya'll would just stay in that basement for the next whoever knows how long until they get home, I might believe it."

"Tex! It's not our fault. It's the other assholes' faults!" Fiona exclaimed.

Tex sighed. "Okay, Fee, you're right. Jess?"

"Yeah?"

"Put the black thingie back in the side pocket of your purse and zip it up again. Make sure you take your purse with you whenever you go out...okay?"

Jess did as Tex asked, feeling a warm glow inside. Kason had wanted to make sure she was safe. It should've felt creepy, but instead it just felt good to know he cared that much.

"Now, pull out your phone, it's why you guys called me in the first place." He waited until Jessyka told him it was done. "Go to your contacts and look for my name.'"

Jess scrolled through, cursing when she accidently pushed too hard and pulled up a different contact. "Damn phone." Finally she made it to the T's and turned the phone around as if the girls would be able to read it from where they were sitting and as she drunkenly wiggled it around in the air. "Hey! Look guys! Tex is already in my phone!"

Tex just sighed over the connection. "Yeah, Benny programmed it in. Now you know. If you need anything, you call me. Okay?"

"Yeah." Jess said it distractedly, thinking about when Kason might have taken her phone and programmed Tex into it without her knowing.

"Summer!" Tex barked out unexpectedly.

"Yeah?" Summer responded immediately.

"What's my number?" Tex demanded.

Summer immediately recited ten numbers back to him.

"Fiona, your turn."

Fiona dutifully also told him what he wanted to know, without looking up the number in her contact list.

Tex did this again with Caroline, Cheyenne and then Alabama. All three women didn't hesitate and repeated his number back.

"Memorize my number, Jess," Tex said seriously. "It's important. People today don't bother to learn anyone's number anymore. What would you do if you didn't have your phone but you needed to call someone? You'd be in trouble, that's what. I'm going to call you back tomorrow night and you had better know it. I'm serious, Jess."

"He *is* serious," Cheyenne whispered in a stage whisper that was more of a shout than a whisper. "He did the same with me and when I couldn't immediately give it to him he sicced Dude on me. And while I love what my man does to me, I don't particularly like punishment spankings. I prefer the erotic ones."

Jess looked at Cheyenne in disbelief.

Cheyenne giggled. "Too much information?"

"Jesus. Okay, I'm hanging up. Ya'll had better not be planning on going anywhere tonight, you're way too blitzed."

"Don't worry, Tex, we're stayin' in," Caroline reassured him. "Thanks for talking to us. We love you!"

The other women all joined in the Tex lovefest until he finally hung up laughing.

"Is he really going to call me tomorrow?" Jess asked in disbelief.

"Yes!" all five women said at the same time.

"We'd better start practicing now so you have it down!" Cheyenne was completely earnest with her words.

They spent the next two hours laughing and giggling. Jess learned Tex's number both forward and backward. Everyone agreed that her plan to recite it to him both ways the next night was genius.

Finally they wound down. Jess thought the night had been a blast.

"Thanks, you guys, for inviting me."

"Thank you for coming over. We know we can be a

149

bit over the top sometimes, but we love our men so much and we're so lucky they all found cool as shit women. Can you imagine if one of us was stuck up and a pain in the ass?"

Everyone laughed at Caroline's words, thinking about how awful it would be if one of them was mean.

Just as everyone was falling asleep, Fiona said into the darkness of the room, "It's not fun being taken and not knowing if anyone knows where you are. You hit the nail on the head tonight, Jess. To know we have a man who'd do anything to protect us, to go so far as to want to make sure someone knows where we are every minute of every day just so they know we're safe? It's a dream come true and probably one of the only reasons we're not curled into a fetal position on the floor, as you so elegantly put it. I'm sure other people would think it's creepy and wouldn't understand at all, but we all agree that it makes us feel safe instead of stalked."

Jessyka was amazed at the amount of recall Fiona had of her words earlier that night. Her impression of the woman went up a notch, and it was already pretty high.

No one said a word and one by one they all fell asleep. Secure in the knowledge that while their men might not be in the same time zone, or even the same country, they were still being watched over by their very own guardian angel named Tex.

Chapter Twelve

ALL SIX OF the SEALs let out a breath of relief as their plane touched down. They'd actually completed a mission without hearing from Tex that one of their women had been kidnapped, lost, tortured, or somehow otherwise hurt.

It seemed as if things were calming down for the group, and the men were thankful. Their women had all been through enough in their lives. It was about time they could just settle down and live a "normal" life.

"Jess found out about what you all did to Brian," Benny commented to Wolf as they were getting ready to de-plane.

"Yeah?"

"Yeah."

"And?"

"She was more concerned about you guys than him."

"You keeping her?"

The question wasn't completely unexpected, and

Benny answered from the heart. "Hell yeah."

"Good. Ice likes her."

"What trouble do you think they got into while we were gone?"

"No idea, but it couldn't have been anything horrible since we didn't get yanked back by Tex."

Benny and Wolf laughed together. As much as Wolf bitched about the trouble the women got into from time to time, they both knew he wouldn't have it any other way.

"We meeting up at *Aces* tomorrow night?" Wolf asked loudly enough so all the guys could hear him.

Before anyone else could respond, Benny asked, "Can I check on Jess's work schedule? I'd like for her to be able to be there as one of us, and not as our waitress."

"Yeah, of course. Sorry, should've thought of that," Wolf apologized.

"No big deal. I'll let you all know in the morning. We'll shoot for the first night she's off, if that's okay," Benny told his friends.

The tarmac was deserted when they got off the plane, no one knew when they'd be returning, so none of the men expected a welcoming party.

The men walked briskly into the small building, ready to get the debrief over with so they could get home to the women who would be surprised, and happy, they were home and safe.

★ ★ ★

JESS THOUGHT SHE heard something and sat up in bed, her eyes straining to see through the darkness of the room. Before she could move or make a plan of action, she saw a shadow in the doorway. Jess threw herself off the side of the bed furthest from the door and landed hard on her hands and knees. The bed sheet tangled around her body and she fought to free herself before whoever it was in her room could get to her.

"Jesus, Jess, it's me."

Jessyka froze for a second, then every muscle in her body relaxed. She recognized that voice. "Kason?"

Then he was there. He picked her up off the floor, tangled sheet and all and sat on the side of the bed holding her in his arms. "Fuck, I'm sorry, gorgeous. Yeah, it's me. We're back."

Jess hugged Kason as hard as she could and buried her face into his neck. Her heart was still beating a million miles an hour. Suddenly she leaned back and smacked him on the arm. "You scared the crap out of me!"

Benny let out a short laugh then got serious. "I'm sorry, Jess. Seriously. I'm not used to having someone waiting for me in my bed."

"You should've texted me and let me know you were back."

"You're right, I should've and it won't happen

again," Benny immediately agreed contritely. He buried his face into the side of her neck and breathed in her unique scent. "Fuck it's good to be back. It's even better to come home and see you in my bed."

Benny relaxed his muscles and laid back on the bed, pulling Jess with him. She sat up, straddling his waist and looked down at him.

"I can't see you. Are you okay? No new holes? Everyone else all right too?"

"No holes, gorgeous. We're all fine. It was an easy in-and-out thing this time."

"Thank God. I worried about you."

"And I worried about you." Benny paused, not knowing if he should really say what he was thinking, then decided he might as well. "It feels good to have someone to worry about and to be worried about in return."

"Yeah."

They lay on the bed for a moment before Benny sat up, taking Jess with him. "Okay, let me up and out of these clothes, then you can give me a proper welcome home... more proper than crawling around on the ground hiding from me."

"Jerk," Jessyka said laughing. "I wouldn't have been crawling around on the floor if you'd let me know you were coming home."

"Uh huh, give me a second and I'll show you how

sorry I am."

Jess moved off his lap and felt Kason stand up. "Hurry up then, I'm feeling a need for you to apologize." She heard him laugh and she scooted up on the bed so she'd be ready for him. Jess peeled off his T-shirt she'd been wearing to bed and waited. The mattress on the bed dipped and suddenly Kason was there.

Jess sighed in relief. She hadn't lied. She *had* been worried about him, and it was the best feeling in the world to have him back in her arms. To be back in his arms. She had no idea how she'd thought for a moment what she had with Brian was love. The feelings she had for Kason were so much bigger. She felt like the luckiest woman ever.

"HEY!"

"Hi, Jess!"

"Yo!"

Jessyka smiled at the greetings she got from the girls. Most of the SEALs just did the manly chin-lift thing, but that was okay with her. "Hey, everyone! Great to see you!" Jessyka walked around and sat in the empty seat at the table. All the guys were there, along with their women as well. It was a lively group, and Jess was happy to be a part of it. She turned and smiled at Kason, who had sat next to her after pulling out her chair.

"Thanks for postponing this until tonight. I couldn't get off before now."

"Hey, thanks for agreeing to come. We know you work here just about every night, I'm sure it's a pain to come on your night off," Alabama told Jess with a smile.

"No biggie. I love this place."

"Hey, Jess, can I take your order?" Jessyka looked up to see Ella, one of the waitresses at the bar standing by the table.

"Yeah, can I get an amaretto sour?"

"Sure thing."

"Draft for you?" Ella asked, looking at Kason.

"Sounds good."

Jess put her hand on Kason's leg. She loved him. She hadn't told him, but she supposed it was probably obvious. They hadn't moved from their bedroom for at least a day after he'd gotten home. They'd ventured out to grab something to eat, but Kason had dragged her back to his bed as soon as they'd finished.

Between bouts of lovemaking, Kason had talked to her about his job, his friends, and about his upbringing. He'd reiterated how he wanted to buy a plot of land when he retired and enjoy his life away from people and their drama.

Jess had even brought up the subject of Tex and the tracking devices.

"The girls called Tex while I was at their house and

brought up the tracking thingies," Jess said cautiously. She didn't want to assume anything.

Kason didn't flinch. He continued to run his hand up and down her back as they lay together, both recovering from intense orgasms. "Yeah?"

Since Kason didn't seem perturbed, Jessyka continued. "He told me about the one you put in my purse."

"Yeah, I didn't have time for more than that before I left. I meant to talk to talk to you as soon as I got back… but we got sidetracked." Kason had grinned at her.

Jess bit her lip. She didn't want to ask. If he wanted her to be safe, like the other women were, then he'd ask her about it.

"Hey." Kason had seen her unease. He turned her on her back and loomed over her. "Are you upset about it?"

Jess shook her head and looked up at him.

"Okay, now's as good a time as any to talk about this." Kason had taken both her hands in his and pinned them above her head. He put his weight on her hips so she was immobile. "You mean more to me than anyone ever has in my entire life. If something happened to you, I don't know what I'd do. I've seen enough evil in my life to be scared shitless at the thought of you disappearing and me not being able to find you. I want Tex to be able to find you with the push of a button if he needs to.

Please tell me you're okay with that."

Jess thought about making him squirm, but the bottom line was she wanted that too. "I'm okay with that."

"Thank Christ."

The sex that followed had been amazing. Probably even more amazing than any other time before... and that was saying a lot. Needless to say, Jess thought it was pretty obvious they had deep feelings for each other. For now she was fine without the words, but she knew she wouldn't be able to hold them back for long.

The conversation around the table at the bar was lively. The guys loved to tease each other about anything and everything. It was a side Jess had never seen, she'd only seen their friendliness and politeness to her as a waitress, and their concern for the women sitting next to them.

The subject of Benny's nickname came up and Jess leaned in, eager to hear the story of how he got it. The other women had shared their men's nicknames with her, but they'd all admitted to having no idea of how Benny got his name.

"So we've been thinking Benny, now that you have a woman of your own, it might be time to change up your nickname," Wolf told him casually, absently running his fingers over Caroline's shoulders as he spoke.

"Yeah, we have a couple in mind, what about Chef?

Or Lock, since you're the fastest lock picker on the team?" Cookie asked Benny, taking a long pull of his beer.

"Sure, either of those would be great," Benny answered enthusiastically.

"What about Stud, or Turtle, since you were the last to find yourself a woman?" Abe teased.

"No, I have it! Sloth!" Mozart joined in, laughing.

Benny was starting to figure out that the guys were just fucking with him... again.

"What the hell ever, assholes," he murmured.

The guys all laughed.

"Face it, you're never gonna live 'Benny' down," Dude said, not unkindly.

"How did he get that nickname anyway?" Cheyenne dared to ask.

"We are *not* sharing that story!" Benny ordered his friends.

Wolf just smiled. "Well, it was one night when we were visiting this crappy bar in a small country in Africa..." His voice trailed off and he got a hard, angry look on his face as he looked toward the door of the bar.

As if in a Monty Python movie, everyone's heads swiveled to see what Wolf was scowling at. Brian had just walked into the bar, along with a group of men.

Jess didn't recognize any of the men that were with Brian, but she shivered anyway. She hated that Brian continued to come to the bar.

"What the fuck is he doing here?" Dude said angrily, voicing what everyone was thinking.

"He comes in all the time," Jess told her friends softly.

Everyone's heads swiveled around to now stare at Jessyka.

"He does?" Fiona asked. "But isn't that… weird?"

"Yes, it's fucking weird!" Benny exclaimed. "Why didn't you tell me?" he demanded from Jess.

"He hasn't done anything. He just comes in with his friends and has a few drinks. I've always avoided serving them and he hasn't caused any issues. He hasn't even talked to me."

"I don't like it," Benny said, frustration in his voice. "I don't trust him."

"Me either," Wolf stated. "Maybe it's time we had another word with him."

"Oh no!" Jess said leaning forward and dislodging Benny's hand from her back. She spoke quickly, trying to head off a confrontation. "It's fine. Seriously, I'd tell you if he did something, but he hasn't. He's stayed away from me. Promise!"

Jess met each one of the men's eyes around the table. She could tell none of them were happy.

"If he says one word to you, Jess, we're going to have another 'talk' with him. We expect you to tell

Benny if he does anything."

"I will, I swear." Jess looked over to Kason. His teeth were clenched and a muscle in his jaw was ticking. She turned to him and put her hand on his cheek. "I swear, Kason. He hasn't really even looked at me since that one time I already told you about."

Benny took her hand off his cheek and kissed the palm before putting it on his thigh and holding it there. He brought his other hand up to the side of her neck and brought her in for a long, slow, and extremely inappropriate for being in public, kiss. When he leaned back, his thumb rubbed against her cheek. "If he so much as fucking looks cross-eyed at you, I want to know."

He watched as Jess nodded at him. "I will."

Benny looked over at the table where Brian was sitting, and caught his eyes briefly, glaring at him, before Brian turned away back to his friends.

Talk around the table was a bit stilted after Brian arrived. Jess sighed. "This sucks. I'm sorry guys."

"Not your fault, Jess," Dude answered before anyone else could.

"I still feel bad. "Maybe I should just go, then you guys can…"

"Shut it, Jess," Abe said. "You will not take this on yourself and we are not leaving."

"But…"

"No."

Abe's voice was hard and Jess knew she should shut up.

Caroline broke the uneasy silence of the group. "So, Jess, did Tex call you after our sleepover?"

Jess smiled at her friend, grateful for the change of topic. "Yeah, he called and yelled at me when I recited the number he thought was wrong back to him. When he figured out I'd just repeated it backwards to him, he was speechless."

"*Tex* was speechless? I don't believe it!" Alabama said in amusement.

"Yeah, he then lectured me for ten minutes straight on why I should be taking everything more seriously. It wasn't until I apologized for the twentieth time that he finally let me off the hook."

The girls all laughed.

Deciding to bring up the topic of the tracers before any of the other women could, and before they could embarrass her about what she'd said at their get-together, Jess commented, "Oh and Kason talked to Tex and he sent the tracers."

"About time, Benny," Dude told him in a low voice.

"Yeah, well, between finding the right time to inform Jess she belonged in my bed and the mission, I didn't have the time." The guys all laughed at Benny as Jess blushed scarlet.

"It's good you got on that. Jess, what're you wearing tonight?" Dude asked, wondering what tracking devices she had on.

Jessyka couldn't believe they were actually talking about this as if it wasn't a big deal. She decided to go with it since she'd brought it up in the first place. She fingered the small gold stud in her left ear. "Well, this is one of them. I've also got one in my purse and Kason drilled a damn hole in my shoe last night and put one there too."

"Don't feel bad, Jess," Cheyenne told her. "Faulkner put one in my bra!"

They all laughed.

"Good idea, Dude!" Mozart exclaimed, then looking at Summer said, "I'll get with Tex in the morning for a new shipment."

"Yeah, me too. Great idea," Benny enthused.

"You guys are all crazy," Jess said without thinking.

"Crazy about our women," Wolf told her seriously. Then putting both elbows on the table he leaned in and Jess couldn't look away from his piercing gaze. She felt Kason's hand on the back of her neck, holding her affectionately, but her attention was all on the man across from her.

"I'm sure you've had a conversation with the ladies and with Benny about this, but let me reiterate something. We don't take this lightly," He gestured around the table to the other men. "There's a lot of evil in the world and we'll do whatever it takes to try to keep it from touching all of you. But if it does, those unassuming little devices will give us a leg up in finding you and keeping that evil from affecting you. Got it?"

"I got it, Wolf," Jess whispered and nodded at him. She'd found it was easier for her to call the guys by their nicknames, except for Kason of course, because that was how Kason talked about his friends and how she'd learned their names.

She continued in a low voice, so no one else in the bar would hear what they were talking about. Jess knew no one else would understand. "And for the record, I'm all for it. I wouldn't have agreed to it if I wasn't. And if I'm ever in a situation where evil comes for me, I'll feel comforted knowing you guys are on your way to get to me."

"Damn straight," Cookie said with feeling, pulling Fiona into his side and kissing the top of her head.

"Whew, okay, enough of the serious talk," Summer said with a smile. "When are we all getting together again to go shopping?"

"You and your shopping!" Caroline laughed.

The rest of the night was spent laughing and joking. The only awkward moment was when Brian and his friends got up to leave. But he didn't once look at their table or act like he knew they were even there.

Jess sighed in relief, glad to have gotten through another encounter with her ex with no drama. She'd had enough drama to last her a lifetime.

Finally Wolf stood up and pulled Caroline with him. "Well, guys, Ice and I are calling it a night. We have the morning off from PT, so I'll see you all in the office."

"When we are having our next ladies' night?" Alabama asked before Caroline was dragged away. Everyone at the table knew why the couple was leaving already, and they all knew they'd all be following suit not too much later.

"How about this coming weekend?" Jess threw out, knowing she had the weekend off.

"Sounds good. See you all here around eight?" Fiona asked.

Eight was a bit early for a night of drinking fun, but they all wanted to be sure to get home at a reasonable hour, because their men liked to keep them up much later, enjoying the effects the girls' night out had on them.

"Perfect! Whose night is it to watch us?" Cheyenne wanted to know.

The guys had decided after Cheyenne, Summer, and Alabama had gotten snatched right under their noses while enjoying a girls' night out, that anytime the women went out, one of them would be there to watch over them and make sure they were safe.

"We'll have to figure it out, but there will be at least two of us here," Cookie said resolutely.

"Okie dokie!" Caroline chirped easily. "See you this weekend!"

After Caroline and Wolf left, the other couples quickly followed suit. They finished up their drinks and the guys paid the tabs.

Jess walked out, held securely against Benny's side. She looked up at him. "I still don't know why they call you Benny."

"And you never will if I have any say about it," Benny said, kissing the top of Jess's head as they walked toward his car.

"Do you want me to call you Chef, or Stud, or Turtle?" Jessyka knew she was pushing Kason's buttons, but it was so fun.

"Not if you know what's good for you," Kason growled at her.

Jess laughed.

On the way home, Jess asked Kason a question that had been nagging at her for a while, ever since she'd found out about the tracking devices. "Does it bother you that Tex knows where we are at all times and you guys don't?"

"No." Kason's voice was resolute.

"Why not?"

Kason looked over at Jess as they stopped at a red light. "It doesn't bother me in the least because I know he has your best interests at heart. I don't give a fuck if he knows you're in the bathroom, at work, at Caroline's, or shopping at the mall. The peace of mind it gives me, gives all the guys, to know if somehow the worst happens and you disappear, we can find you by making a quick phone call to Tex. That's worth him knowing your whereabouts 24/7. There's no one we trust more with your lives than Tex."

"Okay."

"Any other questions, gorgeous?"

"No."

"Good. Because in about ten minutes, if I play my cards right, you won't be able to remember your own name, nonetheless anything about any damn tracking device."

Jess smiled at Kason and ran her hand up her chest until she got to the top button of her shirt. She played with it, swirling her finger around it. Seeing Kason's eyes locked to her finger she playfully said, "Light's green, Chef."

Kason put his eyes back on the road and put his foot on the gas. "Nine minutes, gorgeous."

Jess smiled again and said, "Can't wait."

Chapter Thirteen

BENNY LEANED OVER and kissed Jessyka as if it was the last time he'd ever see her. He pulled back, not letting go, and laughed at the dreamy look on her face.

"You gonna get out or sit here all night?"

Jess opened her eyes and looked at Kason. God, she loved it when he kissed her as if he couldn't get enough of her. "Maybe I'll stay here and you can kiss me again."

Benny smiled at her. "As tempting as that is, you need to get in there and chat it up with your girls. I can't wait to get you home tonight and show you what Dude loaned me."

Knowing how Dude was, because Cheyenne couldn't keep her mouth shut about how well her man gave it to her and how dominating he was sexually, Jess could feel herself grow wet. "Are you freaking kidding me? Kason, that's just mean."

Benny pulled Jess to him again, but this time put his mouth at her ear. "I know you've been talking to Cheyenne so you have an idea of what I mean. I've got a pair of restraints attached to the headboard that have your name all over them. I can't wait to get you home, strap you down, and drive you crazy over and over again until you're begging me to fill you up."

Jessyka shivered in Kason's hold. "Jesus, Kason," she breathed, "Are you *trying* to kill me?"

"No, Jess, I'm trying to make sure you don't forget about me while you're getting crazy with your girls. I'm trying to drive you as crazy as you make me."

"I could never forget you and I think you've succeeded in driving me crazy!"

"Did I tell you tonight how beautiful you look?"

Jess only nodded. Yeah, he'd shown her as well. He'd taken one look at her in her tight jeans and spaghetti strap top and he'd declared they were going to be late. He'd pushed her into their room and proceeded to show her exactly how nice he thought she looked. She was now twenty minutes late and found herself wanting to go right back to the apartment and test out the restraints Kason had borrowed from Dude.

"Well, you are. Every time I think I've seen you at your best, you go and prove me wrong." Benny kissed her one more time, quick and hard, then set her back into her seat. "Go on, gorgeous. Call me when you're ready for me to come and get you. I'll see you later."

"Okay." Jess got out of the car and turned back at the last minute. She watched as Kason rolled down the window.

"Everything okay?" Kason asked.

Jess nodded and took a deep breath. She'd been holding back for too long. If he wanted to get her hot and bothered and leave her hanging, she'd drop a bomb on him too. "I just wanted to let you know that I love you, Kason Sawyer. I can't ever forget you. I think about you every minute of every day and thank God you came to check on me that day in the bar. You're more than just my friend. You're my everything. I'll see you tonight."

Jess backed away from the car, watching as Kason's jaw got tight and he curled his fingers around the steering wheel.

"You'll pay for that tonight," he taunted with a grin as he watched Jess head to the front door of the bar.

"I'm counting on it, Chef!" Jess called back, smiling at him. She felt great. She'd finally told Kason what was in her heart and he hadn't thrown it back at her.

She heard his car leave the parking lot as she opened the door to *Aces*. Jess took a quick look around and sighed in relief at not seeing Brian. He'd been coming to the bar more and more, and it was completely unnerving her.

He hadn't ever said anything to her, but she knew he was up to no good. The SEALs were right to be unhappy that he was hanging around, but she hadn't wanted to rock the boat by having them do something else to Brian. Jess was very thankful to see both Cookie and Dude at the bar. They'd obviously been the ones to draw the lucky straws. Jess felt safer with them there.

Caroline and the others had let Jess in on a secret. The guys grumbled about who would be the ones to watch over them when they went out, but Caroline knew they each coveted the spot. Earlier Caroline had called her laughing because Kason was upset he hadn't won the right tonight and he'd even tried to bribe Cookie and Dude into switching with him and letting him be at the bar tonight.

Caroline had overheard Kason saying that since it was the first girl's night out since Jess and him were together and that *he* should get one of the babysitting spots. The other guys had just laughed at him.

Jess made her way over to the other girls at the round table in the corner. It was the same table they always sat at when they went out.

"Hey guys!"

"Look who finally decided to join us!" Summer laughed as she hugged Jess.

"Yeah well… you know how it goes…"

Everyone laughed, because they did know.

The night was filled with a lot of laughter. Summer and Alabama agreed not to challenge each other to any weird shot competitions, as the last time they did, three of them ended up being kidnapped from the bar.

For the most part, the women didn't overindulge. Maybe they were getting old, but they'd all agreed it was nice to just have a drink or two and girl talk, instead of getting completely hammered.

At one point in the night, talk turned to babies.

"Last week I realized I'd missed my period. I hadn't noticed at the time, but when I did, I was freaking out. I refused to take a pregnancy test until Matthew finally forced me to," Caroline told them ripping up a napkin sitting on the table.

"Are you telling us you're pregnant?" Fiona gasped.

"No. Jesus, no. I wouldn't be here drinking if I was!" Caroline told them. "But it scared the hell out of me. Matthew was the calm one."

"How did he react to you not being pregnant?" Summer asked.

"He was fine, perfect actually. He told me that he wanted whatever I wanted."

"Do you want kids?" Alabama asked.

"I don't know. And that makes me feel horrible," Caroline admitted in a low voice. "I mean, in all the romance books I've read and in most television shows, when a couple falls in love, the culmination of that love is *always* a baby. It's like their love isn't validated until she gets pregnant. Then they live happily ever after. But I'm enjoying my time with Matthew. My parents were older when they had me, and I'm just not convinced it's what I want." She paused a moment, then looked up at her friends. "Does that make me a horrible person? I feel so selfish."

Summer got up and walked around the table until she was standing next to Caroline's stool. "No, you aren't a horrible person. And you know what, who cares if it's selfish? I mean seriously, who says women have to have kids when they get married? Where is it written that a couple's love isn't 'solid' unless they have a rug-rat or two running around? You guys need to do what feels right to the both of you."

Caroline leaned her head against Summer's shoulder. "Thanks, Summer, you always make me feel better. What about you guys?"

No one said anything for a moment. Then Cheyenne shared her thoughts. "I know I'm relatively new to your group, but I agree with you Caroline. I love Faulkner so much. I want him all to myself. All the time. I can't imagine having to give up one second of my time with him right now. I love how we are together and I can't imagine giving that up. But, I think I do want kids—someday. I know how protective and loving he is with me, and I'd love to see him with his child."

"I agree, the press and social media today make it seem like we are complete selfish bitches and not a normal member of society if we don't want kids. What right does anyone have to tell us that we should be popping out babies as soon as we get with a guy? Aren't there enough unwanted kids out in the world already? I should know, I was one of them." Alabama finished huffily.

"To no kids!" Fiona raised her glass. "At least until *we're* ready, and not when everyone else says we should be ready!"

"To no kids!" Everyone shouted and took a big swallow of their drinks. Summer walked back around to her seat at the table.

"Hey, who wants to try an experiment?" Jess asked everyone after a moment.

"Hell yeah, what kind of experiment?" Cheyenne asked eagerly.

"Everyone has their phones right?" When everyone nodded, Jess continued. "Let's send a text to our guys and see how long it takes them to get back to us. Whoever's guy is the last to respond has to buy the next round."

Everyone laughed. "Perfect!" Caroline exclaimed. "But we all have to say the same thing, otherwise it wouldn't be fair."

"Good idea, let's see… how about something short and sweet… and we can't ask a question so they *have* to respond," Jessyka declared.

"How about something like, 'It's so hot in here, I

just took my panties off?'"

Everyone erupted into laughter. "Oh my God! That's perfect, Cheyenne. I'm not even going to ask how you thought of that one!" Summer exclaimed. "And we have to show each other what our guys say in response too!"

"Okay, but since Hunter and Faulkner are at the bar, Fiona, you and Cheyenne will need to go to the restroom, so they'll really think you did it."

"Good idea, Jess. Come on Cheyenne, let's go!"

The other girls watched as Cheyenne and Fiona tripped across the room toward the bathroom. Neither was surprised when Faulkner casually got up and stood in the hallway that led to the bathroom. The last time Cheyenne went to the restroom in a bar, she disappeared. Faulkner wasn't going to take a chance on that ever happening again.

The girls left the restroom and laughed hysterically after seeing Faulkner standing there watching them.

They came back to the table and continued to giggle uncontrollably.

"Okay, everyone get your phones out, but try to hide them from the guys at the bar," Caroline ordered. "Type in the message and don't hit send until we're all ready."

When everyone was done typing, Caroline counted down. "Three, two, one, *send*. Okay, now everyone put your phone in the middle of the table. We'll see whose vibrates first."

Everyone giggled as they waited. Then Cheyenne's phone suddenly wiggled on the table.

"Why am I not surprised?" Caroline said laughing and rolling her eyes.

Cheyenne picked up her phone and everyone watched as she blushed furiously.

"What did he say?" Alabama asked, leaning toward her.

Cheyenne turned so her body was blocking her actions from her man sitting at the bar and showed Faulkner's return text.

Did I give you permission to remove them? Hope you're comfortable sitting on that stool because I'm taking you over my knee when we get home.

"Jeez, Cheyenne, you lucky bitch!" Caroline said, completely serious.

Cheyenne giggled and put her phone back into her pocket. "I know you guys know how Faulkner is with me, but I swear I've never been happier."

Caroline put her hand on Cheyenne's and said seriously, "Just because he's a bit more dominant in bed with you than our guys are with us doesn't make it wrong. If you guys are happy with what you are, who the hell cares what everyone else thinks."

Everyone around the table nodded their agreement.

Suddenly two more phones started vibrating.

Jess leaned over and picked her phone up, read Kason's words, and smiled. "He said, 'Are you ready for me to pick you up yet?'" Jess typed out a short negative return text and put her phone away. "What did Cookie say Fiona?"

Fiona laughed and showed everyone the phone.

What game are you girls playing?

They all laughed and turned and waved at the two men at the bar. Hunter had seen them laughing and he and Faulkner had obviously shared that they received the same text.

"Three more to go!" Jess said with glee. She couldn't remember when she'd had a better time. It'd been a long time since she'd hung out with girlfriends.

The next phone vibrated and Caroline snatched it up. She threw her head back and laughed and showed them all Matthew's response.

Fuck I love girl's night out!

They all leaned forward and stared at the two phones left on the table. Alabama and Summer both looked ready to jump out of their skin. Finally Alabama's phone vibrated, then Summer's did too, five seconds too late for her to have won.

"Damn! Mozart's gonna pay when we get home!"

Summer said laughing.

Abe's return text had said,

Bet we don't make it home before I can make you explode

and Mozart's said,

You're going to pay for that... in the best way possible.

Everyone agreed that while Summer might have lost the bet, they were all going to be winners that night.

Chapter Fourteen

B ENNY WAITED IMPATIENTLY for Jessyka to text or call him to come and pick her up. The words she'd said right before she'd entered *Aces* for the night, echoed around in his brain. Jess loved him. He'd known it already, there was no way she could respond to him the way she had if she didn't love him.

He wanted to show her how much he loved her in return, before giving her the words back. It figured she'd say them when he couldn't do anything about it.

But Benny had the night all planned. He'd been serious when he'd told her what he had in store for them tonight. Benny had spoken at length with Dude about his lifestyle. And while Benny knew he'd never be a hardcore dominant as Dude was, he found there were aspects of it that he found interesting and wouldn't mind trying out.

Jess had never complained when he'd held her down or ordered her around in their bed. He knew she liked it. Benny figured he'd take it just a step further and see if she also enjoyed being physically restrained. If so, Benny knew they had a lot of fun nights experimenting ahead of them. He didn't need to be in control in the bedroom, like Dude did, and he knew Jess liked to take the reins sometimes, which he had no problem with. But, it was fun to mix it up now and then and try new things.

When Jess had texted him the naughty note about her panties, it had taken all he had not to get in the car right then and pick her ass up and drag her home. He wanted to give her the night out she'd been looking forward to, but it was killing him.

Finally around eleven, Benny's phone rang. He didn't recognize the number, but answered anyway, figuring it had to be Jess.

"Hello?"

"Is this Kason Sawyer?"

"Yeah, who the hell is this?" Benny's voice was curt and impatient. He didn't like getting calls from people he didn't know, but who obviously knew him.

"I work at the bar where Jess and the girls are at. Your SEAL buddy told me to call and tell you trouble's brewing and that you need to get down here. Go to the alley in the back and enter that way. He'll make sure the door is open."

"What kind of trouble?" Benny asked, but the person on the other end of the line had hung up. "Fuck,"

Benny couldn't hold back the expletive.

This is the last time they go to that fucking place by themselves.

Benny thought about calling either Cookie or Dude to verify what whoever was on the phone said, but didn't want to take the time. He knew he was being a dumbass, but all he could think of was Jess. Everything he'd ever been taught in his SEAL training said to wait, not make rash decisions, to get all the intel possible before entering into an unknown situation, and perhaps most importantly, relying on his teammates to help him… but he couldn't wait. Not when it was his Jess that could be in trouble.

He grabbed his keys and shoved his phone in his pocket and raced out the door. He jogged to his car and started it up. Not bothering with his seat belt, Benny threw the car into drive and pealed out of the parking lot toward the bar.

As he pulled into the parking lot, the bar looked quiet, maybe too quiet. Benny had no idea what was going on, but he wasn't taking any chances. He parked his car at the far end of the lot, out of direct line of sight of the door and silently made his way to the alley behind the bar. He pulled his K-bar knife out of its sheath and held it loosely in his hand. He had no idea what trouble he was walking into, but he wanted to be prepared for anything.

Benny saw the back door to the bar and made his way forward. He reached for the handle of the door and pulled, surprised to find it locked. The hair on the back of his neck was standing straight up and he suddenly knew he'd fucked up... huge. Hell, it was as if he hadn't spent ten years of his life learning the basics about dangerous ops. Benny wanted to kick his own ass. He had to get a hold of Wolf and the others immediately. He turned around to head back around to the front to find out what the fuck was going on and to call his teammate, but didn't make it two steps before everything went black.

"HOLY SHIT, JESS, please stop! My stomach hurts so bad!" Fiona begged as they all doubled over with laughter again.

"I can't help it if I see some crazy shit here at the bar," Jessyka defended herself. She'd been telling the girls stories about some of the weird things people did when they were drunk. "There was even this one time when a group of women came in and tried to do a shot from the opposite side of the glass!" That made the girls all double over with laughter again.

"Hey, we were amazing at that!" Summer bragged, knowing exactly what Jessyka was talking about.

"Yeah, you were. You'll have to teach us all how to

do it!" Jess agreed and smiled. She couldn't remember the last time she'd laughed so hard. Feeling her phone vibrating in her pocket, Jess eagerly pulled it out, excited to see what Kason would have to say to her. She'd been ready to go for at least an hour, but didn't want to be the first one to bail.

> *I've got your boyfriend. Don't say anything to the others or I'll kill him. Come outside through the back door.*

Jess frowned as she re-read the text. It said it was from Kason's phone. Was he playing a joke on her?

Kp yr pnts on Kason, Ill be hme sn

She clicked the screen off and lifted her head ready to share Kason's impatience with her friends. Over the last few hours Jess had learned they didn't keep anything from each other, and she loved the openness and non-judgmental attitudes of her new friends.

Her phone vibrated again and Jess smiled and looked down to see Kason's response. She gasped instead. There was no note, only a picture of Kason on the backseat of a car. He was obviously unconscious and there was blood smeared on the side of his face. Trying to figure out if what she was seeing was for real, another text came though.

> *I'll fucking kill him and won't think twice. Get your*

ass outside and if you say anything to anyone, or warn them, I'll know and he'll die.

Jess thought fast. There was no way she could sneak out the back. Dude and Cookie were way too paranoid about that back hallway and door. She also didn't think the girls would let her go to the bathroom alone, and one of the guys would watch them if they did go.

I cnt go out the bk. Hve to go out frnt. Dnt hrt him. I'm cming

Jess tried not to panic. She didn't want to be one of those girls who was too stupid to live. And walking out the door would certainly make her just that. She didn't want to be kidnapped, but how the hell could she do anything differently? Jess knew the guys would figure it out quickly. They had to. She knew Tex was tracking her. She didn't think he just sat in front of his computer and watched their movements all day, but hopefully it would look weird when he did finally take a look to see that she went from the bar to… wherever she'd be taken when she stepped outside. Hopefully it would be to Kason.

What sucked was that no one had ever thought about the *guys* needing to be tracked. It had always been the women. Everyone had always been so concerned about one of *them* being taken again. They didn't even think that one of *them* could be kidnapped or put in danger. All it would've taken is one measly device attached to a piece of clothing, or a watch or a shoe or something, and Kason wouldn't be in this predicament. Hell, *she* wouldn't be in this predicament.

If Kason had a tracking device she would've immediately told Dude or Cookie and they would've taken care of it while she stayed safe, but now she was put into a position where if she didn't do exactly as whoever was on the other end of Kason's phone demanded, she could lose the best thing that ever happened to her.

Jess didn't want to risk ignoring whoever it was that had texted her, because she had no idea where Kason was. She didn't know who was behind the kidnapping. Was it someone from a mission he'd been on? She couldn't imagine the guys being so careless as to let one of their enemies know where they were, but she had no other idea who might be responsible. Jess was scared to death, but knew Kason's best chance was to get whoever it was to take her to him and hope Tex was watching.

You have three minutes. I'll kill him if you aren't out here.

Jess closed the phone without bothering to answer and took a deep breath. Showtime.

"That was Kason," she said to the girls, hoping she sounded normal. "He's waiting outside. Guess he got too impatient and wanted me to call it a night already.

That text got him thinking I suppose." Jess laughed, knowing it wasn't her usual easy-going laugh, but she wasn't *that* good of an actress.

"Don't do anything we wouldn't!" Caroline laughed as she hopped off her stool and came over to give Jess a hug. "We'll do this again soon!"

It looked like she'd fooled her friends. Jess nodded in agreement and hugged each of the women. If she held on a bit too long and squeezed a bit too hard, no one said anything.

"I'm going to go and say bye to the guys."

Everyone nodded and turned back to their conversation. Jess took another deep breath. It was one thing to trick her friends, but fooling the SEALs would be another thing altogether. How much time had passed? She had no idea, but knew she had to step this up.

She limped quickly over to Cookie and Dude. "Hey guys, Kason just texted, he's outside waiting for me. I teased him a bit too much before we got here I think." She looked up at Dude. "Guess that little talk you had with him went over well. He said he has plans for me tonight." Jess smiled up at Dude.

"You all right?" Dude asked, taking her chin in his hand.

Damn, guess she wasn't as good at this acting thing as she thought. Jess closed her eyes briefly and prayed he'd let her go. "I'm good, Dude. Swear. Hell, what can go wrong? Tex has me bugged up ten ways to Sunday. I can't take a step without Tex and you guys knowing where I am, right?" Jess knew she was overdoing it, but she had to try to give them some clue. Maybe Dude and Cookie wouldn't get it right away, but hopefully they'd figure it out sooner rather than later.

"Right. Remember you can always say no and Benny'll stop."

Jessyka flushed. Jesus. Dude was talking about her sex life as if he knew exactly what Kason had in store for her tonight.

Dude chuckled, obviously enjoying her embarrassment. "All right, sweetie. Go on home. We'll see you later."

Jess gave Cookie a hug and wished with all her heart she could say something to these men. She knew they'd take action in a heartbeat, but she couldn't stop seeing the words, *I'll kill him,* flash in front of her eyes or get the picture of Kason lying motionless and bleeding out of her head. She wouldn't risk his life. The guys would find her, and hopefully Kason, soon.

Jess headed for the front door of *Aces,* wondering if she'd ever see it again. She turned and waved at the girls. They wavered in her sight a bit because of the tears in her eyes. Jess beat the tears back. Fuck that. She wouldn't cry. She had to be strong. She had two tracking devices on her at the moment, they'd show Tex, and therefore the others, where she was. They had to.

She opened the door and stepped outside and looked around. Jess had no idea where it was she was supposed to go. Suddenly an arm wrapped around her from behind and a cloth was shoved over her mouth and nose. She struggled, but quickly became overwhelmed from the fumes on the cloth. The last thing Jess thought about before she went unconscious was that she hoped Tex was as good at tracking people as the guys said he was.

Chapter Fifteen

JESS WRINKLED HER nose and turned her head to get away from the horrible stench currently filling her nostrils. When the smell didn't abate, she brought her hand up to smack whatever it was away, but her hand was caught in a harsh grip and forced to her side.

Finally she opened her eyes and looked into the brown eyes of her ex. He was holding a little white capsule under her nose that was emitting a noxious smell.

"Brian," she breathed.

"Yeah, it's me, babe. Glad to see me?"

Jess struggled in his grip. "Let go."

"You're going to do exactly as I say if you want your precious SEAL to live. Got it?"

"Where is he? What did you do to him?" Jess refused to give in to Brian ever again. Maybe it wasn't the smartest thing to do, but fuck it. She was done cowering from him. She'd heard all about what Caroline and the other women had been through, and if they could be brave, so could she.

"I've only done to him what his friends did to me. I've been waiting for this moment for a long time. Come on, crip, let's go."

Brian hauled Jess to her feet and kept a strong grip on her arm. She swayed, still trying to fight the effects of the chloroform.

"Now, you're going to walk, bitch. I've hidden him out in the woods so he wouldn't cause any trouble. I didn't want his asshole friends to find him before I was done with him… and you."

Brian pushed Jess toward the trees next to where he'd parked. It was the same park Kason had brought her to in the past when he wanted to talk. Jess bit back a bitter laugh. How ironic.

She stumbled over the uneven ground and tried to keep her pace up. Brian had a light on his hat to help him see as he walked, but Jess had to rely on the meager light coming from it to show her the way. Every time she faltered, Brian would shove her. She fell each time he put his hands on her. The uneven length of her legs had never made hiking easy, and walking through the woods in the middle of the night, and not on an established path, wasn't making it easier.

She fell for the tenth time and Brian brought his foot back and kicked her in the hip, hard. "Get the fuck up, bitch. Swear to God, I have no idea why I wasted so much of my time with you."

Trying to ignore the pain in her hip, and to give it time to stop throbbing before she had to use it again, Jess asked, "Why *did* you Brian? If you hated me so much why the hell did you ask me to move in?"

"Tammy needed a fucking babysitter. You were there. So we decided you'd do."

Jess stared at Brian in disbelief. "You decided I'd *do*? That's all I was? A means to an end for you?"

"Yeah, that's all you were. A means to a fucking end. Then the stupid bitch killed herself. We were making good money off of her too."

"What?" Jess breathed, not believing what she'd heard.

Brian squatted down next to Jess, smiling evilly. "Yeah, she was a good fuck for my buddies. They paid us in drugs and they got… teenage pussy. Too bad she was so fat though, we could've gotten double if she wasn't such a fat ass."

Jess saw red. She had no idea Tabitha was being abused. None. She'd trusted Brian. She hadn't really liked him much at the end, but she had *no* idea he was so twisted. Jess reached out and shoved Brian as hard as she could. "She was your niece! How could you *do* that? That's *sick*!"

Brian stood up and hauled Jessyka up by her hair. As she scrambled to get her feet under her and to take the pressure off her scalp, Brian put his face to hers and sneered, "All she was good for was fucking. I got my drugs and she got some dick. Besides, who do you think came up with the idea anyway? Yeah, her fucking mother. Don't put this on me, Jess, I was just doing what mommy dearest wanted."

Jessyka felt sick. She'd lived with Brian for years. She had no idea Tabitha had been going through what she had. No wonder she'd ended her life. It hadn't been because Jess was moving out, but she'd ended up being more of a catalyst for Tabitha getting the courage to end her own torment. Hell, for all Jess knew, Brian was telling Tabitha he'd hurt *her* if she didn't comply.

"Now, *walk*. Or I'll drag you the rest of the way by your fucking hair."

Jess knew Brian would do exactly as he threatened. She'd never been so scared of him as she was right now. Before, she'd only been worried he'd smack her around. But now? Knowing how depraved he was? Knowing what he'd done to Tabitha? Jess was terrified. Where was Kason? What had Brian done to him? For the first time Jess realized that Brian might have already killed him. He was obviously crazy enough.

Jess stumbled along in front of Brian as best she could. Her hip hurt worse than it had in a long time. Brian kicking it certainly hadn't helped. The pain reminded her of the one time she'd decided she could do a 5K charity walk. She'd done it, but her hip had hurt for at least a week afterwards. The difference in the length of her legs didn't allow her to walk for long periods of time, nonetheless a forced march over uneven ground like this.

While Jessyka fell a few more times, Brian didn't kick her, he just hauled her up time and time again and forced her to keep walking.

Finally Brian came to a halt and grabbed Jess's arm. He pointed to the right as if he knew exactly where he was going. "In there."

"What? Where?"

Brian pushed her hard until Jess fell on her hands and knees. "*There*."

Jess lifted her head and saw Brian pointing toward a break in the trees. How the hell did Brian know where they were going? There was no difference that Jess could see from where they'd just came from and what the trees looked like ahead of her, especially in the dark. She had no idea how far they'd come either. Her faltering gait was misleading. It could have been one mile or four.

Jess stood up slowly, repressing the groan of pain she could feel on the tip of her tongue, and crawled to where Brian was pointing. She moved the branches out of her way and suddenly came face to face with Kason. And he was absolutely livid.

Chapter Sixteen

"**L**OOKIE WHAT I found, SEAL man!" Brian cackled as he propped a flashlight in the crook of a tree nearby. Ignoring the daggers shooting out of Kason's eyes, Brian put his boot on Jess's butt and shoved until she fell with a cry right in front of Kason.

Jess heard Kason grunt and saw him struggle against the ropes that were holding him to a large oak tree. She stared at him in dismay.

Kason had dried blood on the side of his face, obviously from the cut at his temple. Brian had wrapped cloth around his head and shoved it into his mouth so he was effectively gagged. He'd been tied by what seemed like miles of rope. Kason's hands were behind his back, putting his body at an awkward angle as his back couldn't lie flush against the tree he was tied to. His legs had been tied together at the ankles, then wrapped up with the same rope as was holding him the tree at his knees and thighs as well. He also wasn't wearing any shoes or socks.

Somehow it was seeing his bare feet, so vulnerable in the middle of the forest, that got to Jess the most. "I'm so sorry," she whispered before Brian grabbed her by the hair and hauled her upright once more.

"Fuck!" Jess couldn't stop the word from escaping.

"He's not so high and mighty now is he?" Brian murmured into Jess's ear as if he was a lover whispering sweet nothings. "Now he knows how it feels to be helpless, just like I did when his buddies came to visit me. Seems to be a fair exchange if you ask me." Brian threw Jess away from him and she once again landed on all fours in front of Kason. She was sick of being on the ground.

Jess thought fast. She had to do something. Brian was bat-shit crazy. She didn't want to think about what he was going to do to them. She had to buy some time. Jess knew there was no way she could save them both, but all she had to do was give the others time to find them. She wasn't a SEAL, she wasn't a soldier. Hell, Brian outweighed her by a lot and she couldn't overpower him. But maybe she could trick him somehow.

Kason was the vulnerable one here. She knew he was a SEAL and a super soldier, but seriously, he was trussed up so tightly there was no way he was getting loose. Hell, if he could've gotten loose, he would've while Brian was back at the bar grabbing her. It was up to her to save him. The tables were turned for once. It was up to her to protect Kason until his friends could get to them. And she had no doubt they would. It was what they did. She only had to give both her and Kason time for that to happen.

The terror Jess had been feeling since she realized it was Brian that had taken both her and Kason melted away and a feeling of calm came over her. She had no idea if this was what happened to Kason and the others when they were on a mission, but she was going to go with it.

Jess looked up at Kason again and mouthed, "I love you," then turned back to Brian. Ignoring the sounds coming from Kason, she said, "Brian, seriously, why didn't you just talk to me before all this? Do you really think I wanted to hang around Tabitha? Seriously? She *was* fat. It was actually a bit embarrassing to go out with her. Do you know how much she'd eat? Jesus, I was actually a bit impressed. I only hung out with her because I was trying to do what I thought *you* wanted me to."

Brian didn't look convinced. Jess kept talking, staying on the ground and trying not to look aggressive at all.

"You know the day she took all those pills? I brought them to her." Jess's stomach rolled at the lies she was telling Brian, but she *had* to get him to believe her. "We'd talked about it. Oh, she never told me she was having sex with your friends, but she said she was thinking about seeing if taking the pills could make it better for her. I might have egged her on a teensy bit."

Jess could feel Kason's eyes boring into the back of her head, but she continued on. "I told her that maybe if one pill made the sex better, taking more would make it feel even better. She asked me how many she should take and I told her to take the whole fucking bottle."

At Brian's look of disbelief she rushed on. "I know, it's absolutely ridiculous, but she trusted me and believed me. I told her to take them as soon as I left so they'd be able to go into effect by the time your friends got there. She wasn't that smart."

"You always said she *was* smart," Brian said dead-pan.

"Well, yeah, because I didn't want to offend you. She *was* your niece! If you had just *told* me she was your ticket to the drugs, I might not have encouraged her so much. But you were the one who was always complaining about her. I thought I was doing you a favor!"

Jess tried not to throw up. She silently sent a prayer up to Tabitha asking for her forgiveness for the absolute filth that was coming out of her mouth. Jess couldn't think about what Kason thought about her right now, she just kept talking.

"And really, Brian, now that I've had it rough with him," Jess pointed over her shoulder with her thumb at

Kason, "I get it. I get what you like now. I like it. I want it like that with you. We were always so sweet and vanilla. I bet that's not how you *really* like it is it?"

Jess's heart was beating hard in her chest. She was getting to the meat of her plan and it could go wrong in a big way if she wasn't careful.

Seeing Brian's eyes light up in interest and lust, Jess forged on. "Yeah, I bet you like to tie your women up don't you? He tied me up once, and I liked it. I know you like to hold me by my hair, but I haven't done that in the bedroom before. Bet I'd get off on it."

Jess reached behind her and under her shirt. She unsnapped her bra and kept talking as Brian's eyes followed her movements. "I haven't ever tried drugs either. I bet that makes it even hotter, doesn't it? Does it make you feel like you're floating?" Jess pulled her bra strap down one arm and took her arm out of the strap, keeping herself covered by her shirt as she moved. "Have you and your friends shared a woman before? That's another thing I haven't done yet either. Kason's been too possessive. But I bet your friend's hands would feel good on my tits as you shove your dick in me."

Jess pulled her other hand out of her bra strap and pulled the bra off completely. She dropped it behind her on the ground, once again ignoring the furious sounds coming from Kason. She was breathing hard. Jess had no idea if she would get out of this in one piece, but she had to try. She arched her back and put her hands on her hips, making sure to pull her shirt taut at the same time, showing off her nipples, which were clearly visible in the cool night air against the stretched tight cotton. Jess slowly stood up, still talking.

"Have you done that, Brian? What about an unconscious girl? What is it called? A roofie? I bet that'd be fun. Imagine being able to do whatever you want with someone and they can't complain about it. I can't say I want to be the one drugged though, I'd rather watch." Jess laughed, hoping it didn't sound to Brian as fake as it did to her own ears.

"What are your fantasies, Brian?" Jess held her breath. This could go wrong so quickly, but dammit she had to do something.

"I fantasize about fucking you right here in front of this asshole. I want to shove my dick down your throat until you're choking on it, testing your gag reflex. Would you like that, Jess?"

Jess gulped. Fuck. "Oh yeah, you know I've always loved your dick. What else? You'd like it if I fought, wouldn't you?"

"Oh yeah, because when you settled down and accepted the inevitable, it'd be perfect."

"What about if you had to chase me first?"

The sounds coming out of Kason were nonstop now. He was grunting and obviously trying to talk, but

Jess ignored him. It looked like he figured out her plan and wasn't happy.

"You think you can outrun me, Jess?" Brian asked with a sneer. "You're a cripple. You wouldn't get five steps before I'd be on you."

Jess lifted her arms and gathered her hair on top of her head, making sure to arch her back at the same time. She knew her breasts were jiggling under her shirt and fear was making her nipples peak. She threw her hip to the side, ignoring the twinge of pain the action caused.

"Of course I can't outrun you. You know how badly I walk and run with my hip. But you could give me a head start… make it more exciting for you."

Jess held her pose, but rejoiced inside as Brian actually considered her words. She tried to sweeten the pot a bit. She lowered her arms and put her hands on her hips again. "Tell you what, you give me a two minute head start. You can watch which way I go. If you catch me in two minutes, I'll let you and your buddies fuck me at the same time, as long as you share your drugs with me."

"And if it takes longer than two minutes?"

Jess wanted to jump up and down like a little kid, even though she knew she was still in deep shit. She had him. Brian was going to go for it.

"Then your buddies are out, but I'll let you stick your huge cock down my throat right here in the woods."

Jess couldn't come up with anything else at the moment. Hopefully Brian was cocky enough to believe he'd be able to get her within the original two minute time frame. And more hopefully, Tex and Kason's friends would hurry up and get to them.

"Oh, you'll take my cock, Jess, whether it takes two minutes or two seconds."

Jess smiled what she hoped was a seductive smile at Brian.

"Looks like your boyfriend isn't too pleased with you."

Jess didn't want to turn around and look at Kason. She was disgusted with her own words, she could only imagine what Kason thought. But knowing Brian had pointed it out because he wanted her to look, she turned.

The fury on Kason's face, Jess expected to see. His eyes were blazing with it. His toes were curled and every muscle in his body was taut. But under the fury, Jess saw the concern, compassion, and even love in his eyes. She quickly turned back around. Shit. She couldn't do what she needed to if she kept looking at Kason. She needed to stay removed from it all.

"So, want to play catch-me-if-you-can?"

Brian cocked his head at her and said, "You know, I regret not talking to you now. If I'd only known what a kinky little whore you were, we would've gotten along much better."

Jess smiled and winked at Brian, but didn't say anything.

"Yeah, sure, I'll bite. I have nothing to lose. You aren't getting away from me on that gimp leg. It's gonna feel so good to hear you scream as I take you, Jess. You always were a limp fish lying under me, so still. I can't wait to feel you squirm as I take what I want, how I want, and whenever I want. Your two minutes start... *now!*"

Chapter Seventeen

WOLF SMILED OVER at Caroline who was sitting in the seat in his car next to him. She was tired from the alcohol she'd drank that night with her friends and she turned her head to look at him.

"I love you, Matthew."

"I love you too, Ice. Have a good time?"

"You know I did."

Wolf put his hand on Caroline's thigh and moved it slowly upward. "Tired?"

Caroline put her hand over his as it moved up her body. "Never too tired for you."

They smiled at each other until the light turned green and Wolf had to turn his attention back to the road.

His phone vibrated in his pocket and Wolf leaned to the side. "Ice, can you grab my phone and check to see what that text is about?"

Caroline groped Matthew's butt as she pulled his phone out of his back pocket. She smiled as he groaned and said under his breath, "Watch it, or you'll pay for that later."

She smiled and looked down at the phone. She swiped the face of the phone, put in Wolf's password and clicked on the text message. It was from Tex. Caroline frowned, it was late in California, but it was *really* late in Virginia.

"Who's it from?"

"Tex."

Wolf sat up in his seat, losing the easy going vibe he had going on. "What does he want?"

Caroline read the message and her eyebrows scrunched together in confusion. "I have no idea."

"What does it say?"

What the hell is Jessyka doing in the middle of Brant park?

The phone in Caroline's hand started ringing. She startled and almost dropped it, but then immediately handed it over to Matthew, knowing something was wrong.

Wolf took his phone and seeing it was Abe, swiped it to answer the call.

"What?"

"Did you get a text from Tex?"

"Fuck. Yeah, you too?"

"Yeah."

"Call Cookie, I'm calling Dude. We'll see if they know what Tex is talking about."

Wolf ended the call and took the time to ask Caroline a quick question before he called Dude. "Jess was there tonight, right?"

"Yeah, she left around eleven." Caroline looked at her watch, "About forty minutes ago. She said Kason texted her and was anxious to get her home. She said goodbye to us and the guys, then left out the front door."

Wolf didn't respond, but quickly clicked on Dude's number.

"I got it too," Dude said by way of greeting.

"Did you sense anything weird when Jess left tonight? Ice said she got a text from Benny and decided to leave."

"Not really, or I wouldn't have let her leave. But given what's going on now, she did comment on how she was all bugged up and that Tex could find her if he needed to."

"She knew," Wolf deducted quickly.

"Yeah, that's what I'm thinking," Dude agreed.

"Why wouldn't she just tell you guys something was wrong?" Wolf didn't understand what Jess had been thinking.

"What if the text she received wasn't really from Benny?"

"Fuck."

Wolf turned the wheel and guided his car into a large parking lot. He did a wide U-turn and headed back to the street. "Head back to the bar, we'll meet there. I'll try Benny, then Tex."

Wolf clicked off the phone without bothering to say goodbye. Caroline was silent next to him. He took the time to silently run his hand over the top and back of her head to reassure her, then pulled up Benny's number.

The phone rang, and went to voice mail after four rings. "Fuck." Wolf didn't bother trying again. If Benny didn't answer, something was horribly fucked up. He pushed the number for Tex.

"I haven't been able to get a hold of Benny," Tex said as he answered the phone.

"Me either. I've got the guys, we're meeting back at *Aces*."

"Okay, everyone's about the same distance away. I take it Jess shouldn't be in the middle of Brant Park?"

"Fuck no."

Wolf could hear Tex tapping on computer keys in the background. "Okay, she's moving deeper into the woods. Looks like she's headed smack dab to the middle of the park."

"Keep me updated, call me if something changes."

"Will do."

The connection was cut.

Caroline whispered from next to Wolf. "What's going on, Matthew? Did someone take Jess?"

Wolf sighed. "Yeah, Ice. I think someone took Jess."

"I don't understand. Did she walk outside knowing someone was out there?"

"What would you do if someone threatened me, and told you if you didn't go with them, they'd hurt me?" Wolf knew what Caroline's answer would be, and wasn't really expecting her to answer.

Caroline looked at Matthew in horror. "Oh my God. We didn't even think about that."

"Yeah," Wolf agreed grimly and pushed the gas a little harder. The team had to figure this shit out, and quickly. Not only was one of their women in danger, it looked like their teammate was as well.

JESS RAN AS fast as she could. She knew she wasn't moving quickly enough, but the further she could get away from Kason, the better chance Tex and his team had of getting to him before Brian could get back and hurt him after dealing with her.

The branches scratched Jess's face as she blindly ran in the dark. She'd started out running in the opposite direction from where Brian had left the car, then as soon as the leaves had obscured her from Brian, she turned ninety degrees and changed direction. She did this once more until she hoped she was headed back the way they'd originally come. Jess had no idea where she was, or even how far it was. All she cared about was keeping as far ahead of Brian as she could.

When Brian got a hold of her he was going to hurt her. Jess knew it, she wasn't an idiot. But she also knew if Brian took the time to do all the things she'd taunted him with, that meant that Kason would have a better chance of getting free or being rescued by his team.

There was no way she could keep ahead of Brian, but if she zig-zagged enough, and tried to hide more than run, maybe, just maybe she'd buy herself, and Kason, enough time.

Jess couldn't believe Brian and Tammy were as cold-hearted and psychopathic as they were. She refused to cry about Tabitha now. How scared and confused the girl must've been. Shaking her head, Jess tried to put it out of her mind. She had to figure out how to get both her and Kason out of the current mess they were in. She'd grieve later... if she had a later.

Jess had purposely left her bra behind because she knew it had a tracking device in it. The strip tease had done its job in distracting Brian, but it had also been the only way she could think of to be able to leave a tracking device behind for Kason. Jess also had a thingie in her shoe, but there was no way she could leave her shoe behind, especially since she had to run through the damn woods. It had to have been her bra.

Jess fell for the fourth time, but immediately forced herself to get up. She had to keep moving. She couldn't stop. Every painful step meant she was one step, hopefully, closer to rescue, but most importantly, one step further away from Kason and the danger he was in from a pissed-off Brian.

WOLF PULLED INTO the parking lot of *Aces* and slammed on the brakes. He put the car in park and hurried over to his friends.

"Anything?"

"No, nothing looks out of place here," Mozart said in a crisp business-like voice.

The men huddled together, trying to hash out what had happened when Alabama called from across the parking lot.

"I think that's Kason's car!"

The men all turned and headed to where Alabama had pointed. Shit, they were fucking losing it. They should've seen his car first thing, they'd all been too eager to talk with each other than to scout out the scene first. They had to get their act together if they were going to get Benny out of whatever bullshit he was in. Without touching anything on the car they walked around it.

"Doesn't look tampered with," Abe observed. "But why'd Benny park it here and not directly in front?"

"What if he was lured here too?" Cookie mused.

Wolf took his phone out and called Tex and put him on speaker. "Benny's car is here."

"Hold on."

The team waited impatiently as Tex searched for something on his computer. They all knew time was of the essence. It always was. Every second counted. They all remembered how Cheyenne had been saved. If they'd waited too long, the bombs that had been strapped to her body would have gone off and killed her and hundreds of other people as well.

"Benny received a call from the bar around ten. Call lasted about twenty seconds," Tex said in a brusque voice.

"Okay, so someone lured him here and told him something was going down and he had to keep it on the down-low." Wolf turned in circles, checking out the area as he reasoned out what had happened earlier that night. "He didn't call us, so the person probably threatened Jess in some way." Wolf walked toward the side of the bar. "He didn't want to go in the front door, so he snuck around the side thinking he'd be able to get in through the alley."

Wolf, Abe, and Dude entered the alley while Mozart

and Cookie stayed in the parking lot, keeping their eyes on the women who were huddled together around Wolf's car.

The team searched the alley for something, anything, to give them more information about what had happened to their teammate.

"There!" Abe pointed. They all saw the blood spots on the ground and Benny's K-bar lying open and clean on the ground.

"Okay, so whoever it was, took Benny by surprise. They incapacitated him, then sent Jess a text saying if she didn't go with them, they'd hurt or kill him."

"I have a feeling that's right on, Wolf," Tex said from the phone Wolf was still holding. "I hacked into her phone. I'm sending the picture to Abe that was sent to Jess from Benny's phone."

The men waited, and when Abe's phone vibrated, they huddled around it.

"Dammit!" Dude exclaimed upon seeing the picture of Benny unconscious and bleeding on the screen. "No wonder she did exactly what they wanted her to when she saw this."

Wolf was moving back to the parking lot. "Status on Jess, Tex?"

"She's been stationary for about seven minutes now. Still in the middle of the park."

"Okay, we're headed there now," Wolf told him.

"I'm keeping you live on my phone, let me know if anything changes."

Wolf stalked toward the five women standing near his car. He pulled Caroline into him as he reached her side. "We're going to get them back. I need you guys to go into the bar and stay there. Don't fucking move until we get back. I don't care if you get a text or a call. Don't. Move. Got it?"

Ice hugged her man tightly, then pulled back. "Got it, Matthew. Tex has us. You go."

Wolf loved Caroline. She was tough when she needed to be and practical as all get out. She knew just what to say to calm him down. "Thank you, Ice." He kissed her once, hard, then backed away. He watched as his teammates said a quick passionate goodbye to their women as well, then they turned back to him.

"We'll take my car and Dude's. Let's get this done."

The men nodded in agreement and without a word, split up into the two cars and they all headed toward Brant Park to find their teammate and his woman.

JESS GRUNTED AS Brian tackled her and she landed hard on her knees, then her stomach. The light from the lantern on his hat shone crazily around them. She knew it was only a matter of time before he caught up with her... but she'd made it further than she thought she would. Brian roughly turned Jess over until she was on her back. He grabbed both her wrists in his and braced them above her head. He sneered down at her and Jess flinched away from the light shining in her eyes from his hat.

"Tag." Brian sing-songed and then laughed at his own joke.

"You caught me!" Jess said, still trying to buy time.

"Fucking right I did." Brian pulled Jess to her feet and shoved her in front of him until he got to a sort of clearing. He shoved her and Jess fell on her hands and knees. Jesus, her hands and knees were going to be permanently bruised before this was all said and done. Before she could move, Brian was behind her. He grabbed her hips and pulled her back until his cock rested against her ass. He thrust against her as he described exactly what he was going to do to her.

Jess blocked out Brian's voice, refusing to listen to the disgusting words coming out of his mouth and desperately looked around for something she could use as a weapon. There was a lot of trash in the small clearing… it'd obviously been used as a camping spot for some unfortunate homeless person at one time or another.

She looked to her right and saw the last thing she expected to see in the middle of nowhere. It was part of a cinderblock. Jess had no idea how it had gotten there, perhaps a homeless person had lugged it in thinking it could be used for something, but whatever the case... right now it was a godsend.

If she could only get to it.

Brian pulled her back to her feet by her hair, his favorite way of handling her apparently, and shoved her up against a tree. "I'm going to fuck you right here. You're going to take everything I've got. I'll fill all your holes with my cock, then we're going back to your boyfriend and I'm going to watch as *you* put a bullet in his brain. Then you'll come back to my place with me and I'll tie you to my bed and you'll serve as my little honey pot for my friends. Anytime I want drugs, you'll take my friends any way they want and you'll be fucking quiet about it or I'll arrange for your other friends to die as well. You want that? You want to kill your little girlfriends or their men? I'll fuck them before I kill them too. Defy me, Jess. I fucking dare you."

Jess couldn't breathe. She couldn't think. All she could see was Kason tied against the tree, bleeding from a bullet hole in his forehead that Brian had made her put there. Other images flew through her brain, one after another. Alabama lying dead on the floor, Fiona tied up and begging Brian's friends to leave her alone. Cheyenne, Summer, Caroline. She couldn't even think about the guys. They were her friends. No fucking way was Brian doing this. He was a monster. He sold his own niece for drugs and scarred her so badly she felt she had no way out but to take her own life.

Jess lunged away from Brian, taking him by surprise. She got about three limping steps away when Brian managed to stick out his leg and trip her. Jess fell hard once again and Brian threw back his head and laughed at her.

"Fuck, that was funny. You're still trying to get away from me. When are you going to learn that you're nothing but a fucking cripple, Jess? No one wants you. You're nothing and nobody. Do you think I believed your sob story back there? Hell no, I know you loved that fat bitch. You're mine now and I'm not fucking letting you go again just so you can go to the cops. I'll fuck you, and my friends will fuck you, and you won't ever get away from me again. I'll chain you to the bed and you'll never see the light of…"

Brian's words ended abruptly. He never saw the cinderblock that came toward his face. The last thing Brian knew was his feeling of triumph over the stupid crippled woman who was lying at his feet.

"WOLF, WE GOT problems." Tex's words were sharp and biting. Wolf and Dude had just pulled into the parking lot at Brant Park. There was one other car in the lot.

"Talk to me," Wolf told Tex brusquely.

215

"I've got two marks now. One is stationary in the same place it's been for the last fifteen minutes. The other is moving. It started off heading north, then it turned back and is now coming toward you and the parking lot."

"What the hell?" Cookie said under his breath, hearing Tex's words.

"We'll stick together as long as we can, but if the tracks split up too far, we'll need to follow them separately," Wolf said, already setting out into the trees in the park.

The team agreed, and quickly followed Wolf, flashlights in hand lighting up the area as they started toward the beacons.

"What's going on, Tex? I know you can't see us, but are the marks still doing the same thing?"

"Affirmative. The one still isn't moving, and the other has now stopped too. Head north-northwest from the parking lot and you should run right into whoever has the tracker."

The men picked up their pace. They could run all night if they had to, but it looked like they only had to go a short distance before they'd come across the first tracking beacon that had once been on Jessyka.

The men pushed themselves hard. There was so much at stake. They'd been in brutal life-and-death situations before. Situations that included rescuing their own women, and this situation was just as important as any they'd been on before, perhaps more so. One of their own was in trouble. Not only one of their own team, but his woman as well. The stakes were twice as high.

"Tex?"

"Situation static," Tex told Wolf, indicating nothing had changed from the last time he'd reported in.

Wolf didn't bother to respond, he and his team just kept moving. "Spread out, we don't want to miss anything in the cover," Wolf urged the others.

The men fanned out until they were about ten feet apart, and still moving northwest through the thick foliage, their flashlights moving crazily in the darkness.

It was Dude who found Jess first.

"Here!"

The other men changed course immediately and closed in on Dude.

All five men stopped at the edge of the clearing and stared at the scene in front of them.

Jessyka was there, and so was her ex-boyfriend, or what they thought was Brian.

Dude edged slowly toward Benny's woman.

"Jess? You're safe now."

Jessyka didn't respond. She was crouched by Brian's body, breathing hard. She was holding on to a broken piece of cinderblock with both hands. They could all see the blood that had splattered over her upper body.

It was obvious Brian wasn't going to leave the park alive.

"Jess." Dude's voice lowered and he used his Dominant voice. "Put down the cinderblock."

"No."

The men all looked at each other. Jess's voice sounded off.

"He won't touch the others. I won't let him."

"He's not going anywhere. We'll make sure of it." Dude tried to reason with Jess.

"No! *I'll* make sure of it. I'm not a cripple. I'll fucking show him crippled."

Dude couldn't help the inappropriate smile that crept across his face, but looking down at the woman in front of him and the smashed in skull of Brian, made the smile disappear quickly.

Wolf had eased around behind Jess and Dude met his eye. They didn't want to do it this way, but they had to get Jess out of there. Dude nodded at his teammate.

Wolf came up behind Jessyka and circled his arms around her lifting her upper body up and off the ground.

Jess shrieked and kicked backward, dropping the heavy cinderblock in the process. "No! Let me go!"

"Shhhh, you're safe now, Jess. It's Wolf. I've got you."

"Wolf! He's gonna hurt Caroline. Make him stop!"

Her urgent words made Wolf's heart ache. "He won't hurt her, sweetie. You made sure of that. Come on." Wolf turned Jessyka around so she couldn't see Brian's body on the ground. "Talk to us. We're all here. Tex tracked you. Where's Benny?"

It was as his words snapped her out of wherever her mind had taken her. "Oh my God, Kason!" Jess wiggled in Wolf's arms until he loosened them enough so she could turn and face him. She grabbed hold of his shirt, leaving dark smears of blood on his navy blue shirt, and looked up at him. "Kason! You have to find him! He's hurt!"

"Okay, Tex'll lead us there."

"I'm coming too."

"No, you're not," Wolf had no sooner had the words out of his mouth when Jessyka stepped backward and had turned and started hobbling painfully back into the woods.

Cookie swooped in and picked her up with one hand under her back and the other under her knees. "Come on, Jess, it's obvious you're in pain. Let Wolf, Dude, and Mozart go and get Benny for you. Is there anyone else out here?"

Jess struggled in Cookie's arms. "Let me go, Cookie. Please. Damn, I need to be there. He's so pissed…"

"Jess. Is there anyone else out here?" Dude bit the

words out. He'd stepped over to Cookie and took hold of Jess's chin with his hand, forcing her to look at him.

Jess whimpered and panted hard. Finally she whispered, "I don't think so. I only saw Brian. But I don't know how he got Kason out here. He might've had help."

Dude kissed Jess on the forehead and said quietly, "We'll bring him to you, Jess. Hang in there."

Jess could only nod, then she watched as the three men left the clearing heading into the woods back the way she'd come as she was running from Brian.

Cookie and Abe headed back to the parking lot without another word. Jess laid her head on Cookie's chest and prayed they'd find Kason in one piece. She had no idea if he'd forgive the words she'd said while trying to placate Brian, but ultimately it didn't matter. As long as he was alive, she knew she wouldn't have done anything differently.

Chapter Eighteen

WOLF, DUDE, AND MOZART followed the path that Jess had taken through the foliage. They could see where she fell and how hard she'd tried to keep ahead of Brian. It was obvious she'd been running for her life, and Benny's.

It wasn't too far from where they'd found Jess, and with Tex's directions, that they stumbled on their teammate. Benny was tied to a tree and had almost freed himself. There was rope still bound tightly around his legs, but the bindings that had been wrapped around his torso and the tree were hanging loosely.

Wolf stepped up to him with his K-bar knife and quickly sliced through the gag and the ropes around his torso. Dude cut through the bindings around his legs at the same time.

"Mother *fucker*," Benny spat out as soon as the gag was removed. "He's got Jess. We have to find her."

"We've got her, man. She's safe. Tex called us. We found her right before we got here to you."

Benny eased his legs to the side and leaned over and put his forehead on the ground. "Mother fucker," he said more quietly into the dirt. "Mother fucking fuck-er."

Dude put his hand on Benny's shoulder and squeezed.

Pulling himself together, Benny lifted his head and asked, "Brian?"

"Dead."

"Thank you."

"It wasn't us. He was dead when we got there. Jess killed him."

"Mother fucker." This time Benny's words were a whisper.

"She had a cinderblock in her hand when we found them. Brian was dead. Looks like Jess must've hit him at least a dozen times," Mozart told Benny quietly.

"Is she okay?" Benny asked, immediately climbing to his feet awkwardly. It was obvious his legs had fallen asleep after being tied to the tree for so long.

"She seems so."

Benny took a step, then swore. He'd forgotten his feet were bare.

Wolf sat down and started unlacing his boots. Without a word he took off his socks and handed them to Benny. Benny took them gratefully. It wasn't ideal, but having the wool socks between his bare feet and the rough ground would have to do. They'd done this before in an emergency. Hell, "The only easy day was yesterday" was the SEALs mantra. It was second nature to all of them to do what needed to be done.

While Wolf and Benny got prepared for the trek back to the parking area, Mozart picked up Jessyka's bra from the ground. "Pretty fucking smart," he murmured under his breath.

They all understood what she'd done. She knew there was a tracking device in the lining of her bra and she'd somehow removed it so that Tex could track Benny. If she hadn't left it behind, there's no telling when they would've found him. It looked like Benny probably would've freed himself before the night was over, but the tracking device simply sped up the process.

Benny stood up and without a word, took the garment from Mozart and stuffed it into the pocket of his cargo pants.

They left the area much slower than when they'd entered it, leaving the ropes on the ground for the police investigation that was sure to follow the clusterfuck of a night.

The four men didn't speak on their way back to the car, each lost in their own thoughts. Wolf on how close they'd come, once again, to losing one of their women. Mozart on how thankful he was that they'd decided to tell their women about the tracking devices, Dude about how much he admired Benny's woman, and Benny on how much he regretted dropping his knife when he'd been knocked unconscious, he could've gotten out of the damn ropes holding him to the damn tree way before Jess had been involved. But more importantly, how he couldn't wait to wrap his arms around Jessyka and not let go for days. She'd scared the shit out of him and he couldn't wait to see her for himself, to make sure she was all right.

JESS HUDDLED INTO the blanket Abe had wrapped around her shoulders when she'd settled into the passenger side of Dude's car. Abe and Cookie had stood on either side of her, efficiently guarding her and making her feel safe in the process. Abe called the cops and Cookie called Tex. Tex had heard what had happened in the clearing as he'd been on the line, but he also relayed back to Cookie that Wolf and the others had found Benny and were on their way back to the car.

Jess heard Cookie tell her Benny was all right as if she was in a tunnel and he was standing at the end of it. She couldn't believe it until she saw Kason with her own eyes. She couldn't get the image of him tied to a tree, helpless, out of her mind. Hell, intellectually she knew that didn't even come close to the kind of situations he'd probably been in as a SEAL, but *she* hadn't ever seen him in any of those situations.

She *had* seen him tied to the tree tonight, helpless, and she didn't know how else to get that image out of her mind other than to see him upright and alive and well. She could only see him with a hole in his forehead as Brian had threatened... and until she saw with her own eyes that he was okay, she knew she'd continue to see him that way.

Jess heard sirens in the distance, but didn't bother to look toward the road. Her eyes were fixed on the woods in front of her. She strained to catch a glimpse of Benny and the others. Finally she thought she saw lights winking in the distance. Jess heard Tex tell Cookie that they were almost to them and she stood up.

Neither Abe nor Cookie tried to stop her, but they did wince in sympathy as she painfully made her way to the edge of the forest. Her hip hurt, badly, but nothing would keep her from Benny. She hoped like hell he still wanted to see her after everything she'd said and done.

Finally the lights got closer and Jess could make out the forms of the men coming toward her. She dropped the blanket and made her way as fast as she could toward the bobbing lights.

Benny looked up and cursed. His crazy woman was obviously in pain, but she was coming at them as fast as her limp would allow.

He jogged ahead of his teammates and gathered Jess

into his arms. He pulled her off her feet and buried his head in her neck. "Fuck," was all he could say. Benny knew when his teammates passed him and continued on to the cars, but he didn't care. All he could do was feel Jess's heart beating against his own.

Finally pulling his head back a fraction, Benny put her on her feet and put his hands on each side of Jess's head and forced her head up to meet his eyes. "Are you all right, gorgeous?"

Jess could only nod. She couldn't think of anything to say. She was in Kason's arms. She didn't know if she'd live to be here again, if he'd live to be there again. Finally, she said the only words she could, "I love you. I love you so much."

Benny crushed his lips to hers with a short but intense kiss, then tucked her back into his arms. With one hand on the back of her head and the other around her waist, he picked her up again and started toward the cars and his teammates. Jess's legs bumped against his as he walked, but he didn't give a damn.

Jess knew she should probably put her legs around Kason's waist to help him walk, but she couldn't. Her hip was screaming in pain and the thought of moving it was just too much. So she dangled in his arms and let him carry her however he wanted.

By the time Benny got to the cars, the police had arrived, along with an ambulance and a fire truck as well.

He carried Jess over to the ambulance and motioned with his chin for the paramedic to open the back doors. Benny climbed inside, never letting go of the most important thing in his life. It wasn't until he shuffled over to the gurney in the vehicle, that he loosened his hold.

"Let go, gorgeous, let's let the paramedics look you over."

Jess didn't loosen her hold. "I'm fine, Kason. Promise," she murmured against his chest.

"I believe you, but humor me."

At that point, Jess would've done anything Kason asked of her, so she finally pulled back and lay back on the crisp white sheet.

"Don't leave me?" Jess whispered as Kason stood up.

"I'm not going anywhere. Just moving out of the way." Benny moved up to the very front of the small space until he was kneeling next to Jess's head.

Benny watched as the paramedic asked Jess questions about how she felt and if she hurt anywhere. She claimed she didn't, except for her hip. She explained how one leg was shorter than the other and when she overdid it, her hip would ache.

Sometime in the middle of the examination, a crime scene investigator stuck her head inside the ambulance and asked if she could take pictures of Jessyka. She'd agreed and closed her eyes as the flashes from her camera went off. The crime scene tech took at least a thousand pictures, at least it seemed that way to Jess.

After she finally left, Benny asked the paramedic if he could have an alcohol wipe. He used it to gently wipe the splattered blood off of Jess's face, neck and hands. Finally, once she'd been thoroughly cleaned and the EMT was satisfied that she wasn't in imminent danger of passing away, Benny allowed the man to take a look at his own head.

The wound on Benny's head was shallow and not life threatening, even if it had bled a lot.

After refusing to be transported to the hospital and they'd both signed a piece of paper called an "Against Medical Advice" form that absolved the ambulance employees and medics of responsibility over them if they fell ill, Benny helped Jess shuffle out of the vehicle. As soon as she stood on her own feet by the bumper, he picked her up again and headed back to his friends and the police.

He wanted to talk to Jess alone. He needed to lay her on his bed and just hold her. He'd come way too fucking close to losing her tonight and he needed to feel her skin on skin.

"Benny, Lt. Walker needs your statement. Jess's too," Wolf told him in a soft voice.

Benny nodded, he'd expected it.

"He needs to talk to you separately."

Benny felt Jess's hand convulse against him, then loosen, as if she forced herself to let go. He hated this. Ignoring the officer and his teammates standing next to him, he put Jessyka's feet on the ground and leaned back and waited. Finally her eyes came up to his.

"I'll be right here. You'll be able to see me the entire time. Tell him everything, Jess. It'll be okay." He watched as she nodded and took a deep breath.

Jess let go of Kason and took a step backward. She could do this. She lived through the night, this was nothing in comparison. She might have to go to jail, but she felt comforted in the fact that if she was arrested, Kason and the guys would do what they could to get her a lawyer and hopefully get her out on bail. It scared the shit out of her, but Kason was alive… she could do anything now.

Lt. Walker gently took Jess's elbow in his and helped her over to his car. He sat her down in the front passenger seat of his cruiser and he crouched down in front of her.

"She okay?" Abe asked Benny softly, watching from a distance as the officer spoke with Jess.

"Yeah, she'll be sore for a while. She overworked her hip tonight, but otherwise she's remarkably good."

"She'll probably need to see a therapist after what she did to Brian."

Benny thought about it. Jess hadn't seemed to be traumatized to him, but he didn't really know for sure. "I'll talk to her."

"If she needs someone, she can talk to Dr. Hancock. She's done wonders for Fee," Cookie spoke up.

"Thanks, man." The voices fell away and all Benny could see was Jess. She was huddled in on herself in the cop car and he needed this to be done so he could see to her. He hoped like hell the man wasn't planning on cuffing her and hauling her off to the station, but he didn't know what Cookie had told the cops when they'd been called. But knowing Cookie, he probably explained the situation in a way that Jess would be safe from immediate arrest. Finally the police officer stood up and put his hand on Jessyka's shoulder. He walked back over to the SEALs.

"To put your minds at ease, I don't see any reason to bring her down to the station and arrest her tonight. But, she'll have to come in and give a complete statement. I'll need to get all of your statements as well, but I'm thinking it can wait until the morning. We've taken pictures of her and the crime scene techs are out in the park taking pictures there. Anyone have any objection to coming into the station tomorrow and officially talking with the investigators?"

The men were relieved. It was late. Their women were still at the bar waiting to go home. Wolf had called

Caroline and let her know that Jess and Benny were safe. They all wanted to go home and hold their women.

"No problem, Lieutenant. Thank you. We'll be there as soon as we can," Wolf answered for all of them. He also knew Tex would be gathering any and all evidence to deliver to Lt. Walker as well. What he'd dig up would go a long way toward exonerating Jess and Benny.

"Appreciate that. The crime scene techs should be done with the scene in there…" the officer gestured into the woods, "… soon. We'll see you tomorrow… well, later today."

All Benny could think was, "Thank God." He turned on his heel and headed to Jess. She held up her arms as he came toward her and waited for him to get her.

Benny leaned down and picked her up with one arm under her knees and the other behind her back. Jess wrapped her arms around him, as she had before, and tucked her face into his neck. He carried her back over to Dude's car and got into the backseat. The other men quietly climbed in as well, Abe in with Dude, Jess, and Benny. Mozart and Cookie joined Wolf in his car.

Dude turned on the engine and pulled out of the parking lot and headed back to the bar. Not a word was spoken as they traveled the short distance. Finally pulling into *Aces* parking lot, Dude shut off his car and said, "I'm fucking proud of you, Jess. I don't know all that went on out there, but you obviously used your head and you survived. From what I can tell, you protected Benny. We found the tracking device you left behind, it led us right to him. Good job."

Jess buried her head deeper into Kason's neck and simply nodded, too overwhelmed to even answer the big man in the front seat. His voice had been gentle, but it was still too much for Jess right then. All she could see was the pictures Brian had put in her head that night. Of Cheyenne and the other women, hurting, or dead.

Dude climbed out and opened the back seat of his car for Benny. "You need any help?" he asked Benny.

"I got it. Thanks man. I owe you."

"You don't owe us dick, and you know it."

Benny just smiled at his friend. He settled Jess into the front passenger seat of his car and buckled her in. He kissed her forehead and closed the door. He jogged around to his side, still in Wolf's borrowed socks, and climbed in. He eased out of the lot and headed back to his apartment. He couldn't wait to hold Jess close and forget how they'd both come way too close to being killed or seriously hurt.

Chapter Nineteen

BENNY HELD JESS against his side as he fumbled with the key to his apartment and opened the door. He didn't take his arm from around her waist as he took most of Jess's weight and propelled them inside. He dropped the keys in the bowl by the door and shut and locked the door behind them.

Without letting go of her, Benny walked them to the counter and snagged the small envelope off the counter that held two pain pills left over from Jess's hospital visit the night Tabitha had died. She hadn't needed to use any more after that first night, and Benny had put them in a large bowl filled with odds and ends on the counter.

Benny then turned and made his way down the hallway to the master bedroom. Jess hadn't said a word, she simply clung to Benny's side and went wherever he led her.

He took them inside his bedroom and into the master bathroom. Benny walked her over to the toilet seat.

"Sit, gorgeous, give me a second."

Jess did as he asked. She eased down, with Benny holding onto her waist. Once she was sitting, Benny took his hands away from her and grabbed a cup from the counter and filled it with water. He shook out the pills and held them out to Jess along with the cup of water. She took both without protest and quickly swallowed the pills. She drank half the glass of water before handing it back to him.

Jess watched as Kason turned from the sink and pulled the shower curtain back. She fidgeted on her seat. She couldn't quite read Kason's mood and she was getting worried. She didn't think he was mad at her, but since he wasn't talking to her, she didn't know for sure.

Kason tested the temperature of the water and Jess kept her eyes on him as he then grabbed his shirt and tore it off over his head and dropped it on the floor. He eased the socks off his feet then turned to look her in the eyes as he unbuttoned and unzipped his cargo pants and dropped those to the floor as well. Jess's eyes widened as Kason then dropped his boxer briefs to the ground. He stood in front of her completely naked, the most handsome man she'd ever seen. He was hard in all the right places. He had muscles on top of muscles. Jess was confused, as it was obvious Kason wasn't aroused, and wasn't getting ready to have shower sex. His manhood hung flaccid between his legs. Jess hadn't often seen him when he wasn't turned on, and she wasn't sure what to make of whatever was happening.

Benny knew he was probably freaking Jessyka out, but he couldn't think of anything other than getting her clean and then holding her safe in his arms. The words she'd hurled at Brian tonight kept pinging around in his brain. He knew exactly what she'd been doing and he'd never felt more helpless in his life. He was very rarely helpless, and found he hated the feeling.

When the water was a comfortable temperature, he stepped over to Jess. She hadn't moved, that alone told him she was probably in more pain than she'd ever admit to.

"Arms up," Benny told her in a low voice. Jess immediately complied, and he helped ease her shirt over her head. Once the shirt was removed, Benny held out his hands palm up. "Let me help you stand." Jess wasn't wearing a bra, it was still in the pocket of his cargos, so there was no need for him to help her to remove it.

Jess put her hands in his and he took most of her weight as she stood up. Benny kneeled down, feeling Jess's hands rest on his shoulders for balance, and untied both her shoes and eased them off her feet. Then, still kneeling, he unbuttoned and unzipped her jeans and carefully pulled them down her legs. He tapped her right foot and she shifted until it was off the ground. Benny steadied her as she stood on one foot. He pulled the leg of her jeans off that leg, then repeated the same actions on her other side.

Benny meant to keep everything clinical and medicinal, but he couldn't help himself. Having her so close to him, and in one piece, he couldn't stop himself from reaching forward and drawing Jess to him. Benny lay his cheek on her belly and wrapped his arms around her and rested the palms of his hands on her back. He felt Jess's hands go to his head and gently caress him as he took comfort from having her safe in his arms.

Finally Benny looked up from his crouched position in front of her. "You're okay, aren't you, Jess?" he whispered, feeling raw inside.

"I'm okay," Jess whispered back.

Benny nodded and rested his forehead against the small pooch of her belly for a moment. Finally, he took a deep breath and pulled back an inch. He took hold of her panties on each side of her hips and drew them down her legs. He held Jess steady as she stepped out of them.

Benny stood up fully and wrapped his arm around her waist again and helped her to the side of the bathtub. Not allowing her to step over the deep side of the tub because he knew it would only cause her pain, Benny lifted her bodily into the shower. He closed the curtain after he stepped in with her and eased them both back until the water was hitting Jess's lower back.

He put both hands up to the side of her head and gently tipped it back until the water was running over her head. "Close your eyes, Jess, let me wash away the night."

Benny felt Jess melt into his hold. He gently squirted some of her shampoo into his hand and lathered up her hair. He washed and rinsed her hair twice before working in a handful of conditioner.

While the conditioner was doing its thing, Benny turned Jessyka until her front was facing the warm spray of water. When she went to protest, Benny shushed her with his words. "Let me, gorgeous. Let me clean you."

Jess nodded and Benny squirted some of his body wash into his hands. He needed her to smell like him. He wanted to rub a small piece of himself into her skin. He ran his hands over her chest and belly, then moved to her arms and hands. He carefully ran his soapy hands over her neck and face, making sure to leave not one inch of the skin that had been sprayed with Brian's blood unclean. Squirting more soap into his hands, he then moved to her legs. He briskly cleaned her sex, then rubbed her back. Once Benny was convinced Jess was clean and there wasn't one speck of Brian's blood left on her, he turned her back around and gently rinsed the conditioner out of her hair.

Then while Jess stood in the spray of the water, Benny quickly ran soap over his own body, not bothering to watch what he was doing, he kept his eyes locked on Jess. He took a step toward her and she stepped back until the water was hitting Benny, and not her. After a quick rinse, Benny reached around Jess and turned off the water. He then pulled her into his side again and opened the shower curtain.

He grabbed a towel and dried every inch of Jessyka's body before wrapping the towel around her. He lifted her out of the tub.

Benny watched as she turned to the sink and picked up her toothbrush. He wiped himself down quickly and then wrapped the towel around his own waist. Benny picked up his own toothbrush and followed Jess's lead. When they were ready, he took both their towels and threw them on the floor of the bathroom, not caring if they sat in a wet heap on the floor all night, he picked Jess up as he had in the park. He put both arms around her and lifted her up until her feet were off the ground and clasped her to him. Her front to his front, then carried her into the bedroom. He gently put her down, pulled back the covers and encouraged Jess to climb in. He followed behind her after turning off the overhead light.

It was now nearing dawn. Between the kidnapping, her running through the park, being rescued, and then being questioned by the police, the morning sky was slowly lightening as the sun made its way across the globe.

Benny wrapped both arms around Jess and pulled her to him. She buried her face into his chest and went to wrap one leg around his.

"No, Jess, I don't want any strain on that hip."

Benny put his own leg around hers instead, and pulled her into his body.

They were both quiet for a moment, enjoying the feel of each other's body, skin to skin. Jess broke the silence. "I wasn't sure I'd ever feel this again."

"I can't decide if I want to beat your ass for everything you did tonight or make love to you until the only thing you can feel and think about, is me."

"Do I get a choice? I choose door number two."

Benny smiled for a moment at her words, then got serious again. "Seriously, Jess, I think you took ten years off my life when I saw him push you into that clearing. He threatened to kill you if I didn't do exactly what he said. I bided my time, thinking I'd be able to get away after he got me where he wanted me. I didn't know exactly who was behind tying my ass to that tree, he had me blindfolded as he led me out there, until I saw him shove you to the ground in front of me. What the hell were you thinking?"

Jess didn't even raise her head, but instead snuggled closer to Kason and his arms got even tighter around her. "He sent me a picture of you bleeding and unconscious."

Without letting her continue, Benny barked, "So?"

Jess finally lifted her head at that. "So?"

"Yeah, so? Jess, I'm a SEAL. There's nothing you could've done, as a civilian, to help me."

"That's not exactly true." Jess was getting mad now. "You're not invincible, Kason. No one knew you were gone. No one knew where you were. Only some asshole who took your picture while you were *unconscious* and *bleeding* and sent it to *me*. Tex couldn't find you in the middle of a fucking forest for God's sake with nothing to go on. I knew I was tracked. I knew he could find *me*. I figured if I could get to you, you'd figure something out and Tex could rescue both of us. I didn't know you'd be all tied up without any damn shoes on."

She hiccuped and continued, obviously on a roll. Benny just let her get it out. Jess was so damn cute when she was riled up. He didn't think he'd ever get sick of watching her.

"I knew Brian was an asshole, but I didn't know he was *that* much of an asshole. I did the only thing I could think of. He wasn't going to let me just waltz on out of there. It's not like I could've said, 'Hey, I'm just going to take my bra off because it has a tracking device in it.' Dammit, Kason, what the hell are you smiling at?"

"I love you, Jess."

Jess stopped mid-rant and stared at Kason. Her face

crumpled and she bit out, "Oh fuck."

Benny smiled tenderly at her and pulled her into his chest again.

"I love you so much, Kason. I was so worried about you."

Benny heard her words mumbled in his chest and he put one hand on the back of her head and caressed her.

"I know, gorgeous, I love you too."

"I d-d-didn't know what to do."

"You were amazing."

"You weren't wearing any s-s-shoes," Jess wailed, obviously having reached her breaking point. "They were r-r-raping T-T-Tabitha."

"I know, I'm so sorry."

"I d-d-didn't know, Kason. I swear I didn't."

"Of course you didn't, Jess. I'd never think that about you.

"I made all that stuff up that I told him."

"Jess. Hush. I *know*."

"He was going to go back and kill you. He s-s-said he was going to make me put a b-b-bullet in your head. Then he said he was going to r-r-rape Caroline and fuck the other girls. I didn't want his filth to touch them. I didn't want you to d-d-die." Jess lifted her head and looked Kason in the eye. "I killed him. I hit him with that cement block. Then I did it again. I didn't stop even when he was on the ground and not moving. All I could see was Tabitha, and you, and Cheyenne and the others... I'm not sorry. I'd do it again if I had to."

Benny reached up and took Jess's head in his hands and held her still. He saw her red-rimmed eyes and her running nose. She'd never looked more beautiful. "Good for you. I'm so fucking proud of you, I can't stand it. You didn't back down, you thought on your feet and you did what you had to do. I'm not thrilled you were out there in the first place and that you put yourself out there though. I'm sorry as hell I couldn't rescue or protect you, but you did it for yourself. I fucking love you so damn much."

Benny kissed Jess once, hard, then drew back, not letting go of her head. "I'm sorry you had to kill him, I'd never want that on your conscience, but I'm not sorry he's gone."

Jess bit her lip, then pouted. "I didn't get my night you promised me."

With her words, Benny knew Jess was going to be all right. He didn't see any angst in her eyes at taking Brian's life. He knew it might hit her later and she might feel remorseful, but he was thankful she wasn't broken as a result. He'd still suggest she get counseling until they were both a hundred percent sure she was okay, but for now he was relieved as all get out that she seemed to be okay. Benny kissed her forehead and brought her back into his hold. "You'll get your night, gorgeous. I promise." After a beat he asked, "How much pain are you in?"

"On a scale of one to ten?" Jess asked groggily, snuggling deeper into his arms.

"Yeah, on a scale of one to ten."

"Around a twelve."

Benny made a distraught sound in his throat and made like he was going to get out of bed.

"If you move one inch I'm going to have to hurt you," Jess grumbled, tightening her arms around him. "Yes, I hurt. But all I want to do is lie here with you. Feel you against me. I didn't know if I'd ever have this again. I took the pills, they'll kick in soon enough. I'll be okay. Please, Kason. Give me this. I *need* this. I promise I'll feel better when we get up. I haven't run in years and my body is reminding me why I shouldn't go on long romantic walks or run through the woods away from a crazy psychotic asshole. Please? Just hold me?"

"If it's not better later, you're going to the doctor."

"Promise. Thank you. I love you."

"And I love you too, gorgeous." Benny kissed her on the top of the head. "Sleep. Tomorrow, well later today, we'll start the rest of our lives together."

"That sounds good."

Benny held Jessyka as she fell asleep. He knew they had a lot to figure out in the next few days. The team had to give their statements to the police. Jess would have to continue to deal with the legal ramifications of having killed Brian. Benny didn't think it'd be an issue based on how Brian had hurt her before. Benny also hoped there would be some evidence in his townhouse about his drug activities.

They'd also have to deal with Tammy. If what Brian had told Jessyka was true, she was just as guilty in the pimping out of her daughter as Brian was. Benny also knew Jess would have to psychologically deal with everything she'd learned that night. They'd spent the last few hours hyped up on adrenaline and he knew she hadn't had time to process everything that had happened.

But Benny figured she'd be all right. Everything he'd told her tonight was true. Jess was tough and smart and she'd done well in trusting Tex to bring his team to their rescue. She'd been put in a horrible situation that neither he, nor any of the other guys had even thought about. They hadn't thought someone would use *them* to lure the more vulnerable women into a dangerous situation. They'd have to do some soul searching about that. They'd all thought tracking the women would keep them safe, but it was obvious they'd missed the huge flaw in that thinking. Brian was an idiot, but he'd managed to find the one thing that would present Jessyka to him as if on a silver platter. Jess had done the best she could in a fucked up situation, and the bottom line was that she'd trusted Tex and the rest of the team to get to both of them in time. Thank god they had.

Benny held Jess long into the morning as the room slowly brightened. He watched her breathe in and out and he never felt happier. She was alive. He was alive. They loved each other. He felt like the luckiest man alive.

Chapter Twenty

"**Y**OU KNOW YOU were a bonehead, right?" Wolf asked Benny, completely relaxed with one arm thrown over Caroline's shoulders as they sat at a table in *Aces* a week after Benny's kidnapping.

"Shut it," Benny responded to his team leader and friend.

"Seriously," Dude joined in, not willing to let it go. "I wasn't allowed to go into that basement and get Shy out by myself, I don't know why you think *you're* superman or something and could rush in singlehandedly and save your woman." Dude's words were teasing, but they all knew there was more than a kernel of truth to them.

"Look, I could sit here and give you all a load of shit about how I thought I had it under control and how it wouldn't have been a big deal if I hadn't been taken by surprise, but we all know that's a load of crap. I fucked up. I admit it. I should've immediately called one of you, or hell, even Tex, to see what the situation was. I've been trained better than that. Hell, if anyone on one of my teams did that shit I'd have blown a gasket on them."

Benny looked down at Jess. She had one hand resting on his thigh and he could feel the heat from her hand burning into his leg. He almost lost her. She'd had to do the unthinkable and kill a man, because he ignored all his training and leaped before he looked. "All I can say is that when Brian said that Jess was in danger, I could think of nothing but getting to her as fast as I could."

His teammates all nodded, knowingly. They'd all been there. They understood better than anyone else. "But I've learned my lesson. No more lone wolf shit from here on out. Even if, God forbid, this happens again. We're a team. Always. We all need each other. I won't forget again."

"See that you don't," was Abe's response. His harsh words were tempered with a smile. Benny relaxed, glad the well-deserved ass kicking was out of the way.

"I have no idea how I got so lucky to be sitting here with all of you today," Jessyka told the men and women around her honestly and with emotion clear in her voice. "I mean, I always knew the military was a close-knit group, but I had no idea it'd be like this."

When Caroline went to say something, Jess held up her hand to stop her and continued speaking. "I saw you week after week in the bar. I watched as each of you guys," she motioned to the men, "found a woman who was perfect for you. Abe, you always put the women you dated first, but they obviously didn't care about you. Then you found Alabama. I watched as she made sure you had refills of your beer, she ordered you food when you came to the bar after working all day, she even made you go home before everyone else when she knew you were tired."

Jess watched as Alabama leaned her head against Abe's shoulder and he kissed the top of it and turned his attention back to her. "And you, Cookie. You had to go all the way to Mexico to find Fiona, but you were tenacious in your quest to make sure she always felt safe. In return, she always does her best to give you what you need, whether that be giving you the chair against the wall, or a shoulder rub when you're tense. Mozart, you were suffering. You held a grudge against everyone and it was obvious to see. Summer helped you let that go and cling to love instead. In the end, your love for her was more important than revenge for yourself."

Jessyka hurried to finish. The looks the guys were giving her were going to make her start bawling any second now.

"And Dude, I know you never realized it, but you never used your left hand for anything, you always kept it in your lap. You didn't realize that the fact you only have part of a hand didn't mean jack squat to anyone around you, and if it did, they weren't good enough for you anyway. Cheyenne was made for you. She never saw you as incomplete or wounded. She only sees your heart.

"Caroline, you and Wolf were the catalyst that started all of this." At their looks of amusement she continued. "I know, you think I'm crazy, but I wanted to be just like you guys. The other guys here did too. They saw what a good, healthy relationship was supposed to be like. Shortly after you moved here, the rest of the guys stopped being such horn dogs and started paying attention to what they really wanted in their lives.

"I knew you were all friends, but I thought that was as far as it went. I had no idea that not only are you all friends, you're family as well. I wanted to be a part of this, but never in a million years dreamed I would be, not like this." Jess turned to Kason. "I love you so damn much. I'd do anything for you. I'd walk right into the hands of a crazy psycho every day of my life if it meant keeping you safe."

Benny growled at her and leaned over and lifted Jess into his lap so she was sitting sideways and still facing their friends.

Jess continued talking from within Kason's arms. "I used to think that therapy was for wimps." When Hunter looked like he was going to say something, Jess continued quickly. "And I thought I'd be fine after what happened... but thanks to Fiona urging me, and some soul searching, I've realized that it's okay to need to talk to someone about what happened. My situation is way different than Fiona's, and Alabama's, and Summer's and even yours, Cheyenne, but just because I find talking to the doctor about what I did, and what Brian and his sister did, soothing, doesn't mean I'm crazy or that I'll need to see a shrink for the rest of my life. I have more respect for the eleven of you sitting around this table than I ever have for anyone in my entire life."

Jessyka took a deep breath, glad she'd said what she needed, and wanted, to say before anyone could interrupt her. The couple of visits to Fiona's therapist had helped a lot, even though she didn't think, at first, she needed to see her. She'd most likely continue to see her to talk through everything that happened, but for now, she was good with everything.

"I think, however, that we've all had enough drama in our lives. Can we please, maybe, just live like normal people without being lost, kidnapped, or used for someone's revenge for at least a few weeks? I mean, what else could we go through?" Jess finished exasperatedly.

Everyone moaned and shook their heads.

"Jesus, Jess, you can't say that shit," Cookie groaned. "Seriously, you've just jinxed us."

"No way, we're through. We're destined to live easy-going normal lives from here on out. After all, we've all found men of our own, we're good," Caroline said this as if she was laying down the law.

"That's true. Now that we've found our men and settled down, we shouldn't have any more drama," Cheyenne agreed with Caroline.

"We haven't all found our mate though," Jess pointed out.

"Uh, I hate to burst your bubble, gorgeous, but none of us are letting you girls go. You're stuck with us," Benny said while nuzzling the side of Jess's neck.

"Tex," Jessyka said matter-of-factly. "He's a defacto part of this team too. And from what I understand, he isn't with anyone."

The group was silent for a moment, then Dude spoke up. "Hon, we haven't really sat down with Tex and talked through any of this shit, but he's even more sensitive about his leg than I am with my hand."

It was true. Tex talked a good game when it came to the prosthetic he wore ever since he'd been medically retired from the Navy, but everyone was aware that he joked a little too much about how he was crippled and laughed when women turned him down once they found out about his injury.

"But Dude, Tex is a part of this team. He *has* to find his perfect match. Face it, if we all somehow found each other, he will too." Jess leaned back against Benny, resting her head on his shoulder and her cheek on his chest. She wrapped an arm around his shoulders and idly played with his hair at the nape of his neck. "I don't know how, and I don't know where, but you guys have all said it yourself. Tex can find anyone no matter what. I have a good feeling about this. He'll find his woman, one way or another."

THOUSANDS OF MILES away, on the other side of the country, Tex tapped rapidly on his keyboard.

Mel? Are you there? Haven't heard from you in a while.

After a few minutes with no response, Tex tried again.

I'm worried about you. Please. Talk to me. I miss your sarcasm. ;)

When there was still no response, Tex tried one last time to connect with the woman he'd been chatting with online for the last few months.

If you don't answer me, I'm going to have to do something drastic to make sure you're all right. I know you never wanted to talk on the phone, or exchange photos, but I have to know you're okay. I've already given you my cell number, please call me.

Tex got up and adjusted his prosthetic before walking into his kitchen to grab something to eat for dinner. He brought his plate back into his computer room and glanced over the three monitors sitting on his desk, then he looked over at the GPS coordinates that were constantly displayed on a map. He smiled. All his friends, and their women, were currently at *Aces*, most likely eating and hanging out as friends did.

Tex loved each and every one of them, and he was pleased he played a part in keeping them together. Using his computer and his skills to track people down, made him feel good, when most days he didn't feel very worthy. He'd missed feeling as if he was part of a team when he retired. He lost the adrenaline rush that came from successfully completing a mission when he'd left.

He'd been cut off from everything he'd loved and hadn't had a chance to figure out what he was going to do with his life. The Navy had been his life. But he'd always been good with computers. And between his computer skills and some of the nefarious people he'd met in his life, he'd found his new niche.

If he felt jealous of his friends and the wonderful women they'd found to spend the rest of their lives with, Tex would never let on.

Tex thought back to the conversation he'd had with Jess, Benny's woman, the other night. She'd called to thank him for noticing so quickly something was weird the night Benny had been used as a lure to get her out of *Aces*. She'd ranted and raved at him that it was asinine to only track the women. She'd had a compelling argument, telling Tex that if he'd been tracking Benny the night he'd been kidnapped by her crazy ex, she never would've had to put herself in danger.

When Jess had put it that way, Tex couldn't disagree with her. Thus, the six big bad Navy SEALs he'd gotten to know very well over the last months, were now all owners of shiny new tracking devices.

The men had balked about wearing the trackers when they were out of the country on a mission, but Tex had pointed out that he was the only one who knew about the devices, and it couldn't hurt to have the extra protection when they were in foreign countries doing the dirty work that was too dangerous for most other military teams. They'd agreed to put the devices in their packs as a concession. Tex wanted to point out that packs could be lost or stolen, but the women had been so relieved, he'd dropped it.

Tex turned back to his computer screen, trying to put his friends out of his mind. Hopefully they'd seen the last of the drama they'd all been through over the last year or so.

He clicked some buttons on his keyboard and stared at the chat box he'd just been using to talk to Melody.

User unknown

Tex frantically clicked more buttons, then swore under his breath and leaned back in his chair and put his hands behind his head. She'd deleted her account. She wasn't just logged off, she'd severed the only connection they had with each other.

They'd been talking for months, and she'd never given any overt indication that anything was wrong, but Tex still sensed there was something. Obviously he was right. He knew her well enough to know she was too polite to just up and disappear without a word... at least he thought he did.

They hadn't gotten into anything sexual, but they'd definitely shared some intimate thoughts. Melody was the only person he'd told how useless he felt and how, even though he'd ultimately begged the doctor to remove his mangled leg, he hated the fact that he wasn't whole. He'd even opened up to her about the phantom pain he still felt all the time in his leg, a leg that wasn't even there.

Melody had understood. She'd said all the right things. But thinking about it now, Tex realized she'd never *really* told him anything about herself. Oh, he knew she liked to eat Mexican food and that pink was her favorite color, but she'd never opened up to him about the things that really mattered in her life.

He pushed up the sleeves on the shirt he was wearing and crouched over his keyboard. If Melody thought she could erase their connection as easily as deleting her user account, she had another think coming.

The SEALs always said he could find anyone, it was time to put his skills to use... for himself this time. Something was wrong. He'd find Melody and figure out what it was. Hopefully he wouldn't be too late.

Look for the next book in the
SEAL of Protection Series:
Protecting Julie.

Discover other titles by Susan Stoker

SEAL of Protection Series

Protecting Caroline
Protecting Alabama
Protecting Fiona
Marrying Caroline (novella)
Protecting Summer
Protecting Cheyenne
Protecting Jessyka
Protecting Julie (novella)
Protecting Melody
Protecting the Future

Delta Force Heroes Series

Rescuing Rayne
Assisting Aimee (loosely related to DF)
Rescuing Emily
Rescuing Harley
Rescuing Kassie (TBA)
Rescuing Casey (TBA)
Rescuing Wendy (TBA)
Rescuing Mary (TBA)

Badge of Honor: Texas Heroes Series

Justice for Mackenzie
Justice for Mickie
Justice for Corrie
Justice for Laine (novella)
Shelter for Elizabeth
Justice for Boone
Shelter for Adeline (TBA)
Justice for Sidney (TBA)
Shelter for Blythe (TBA)
Justice for Milena (TBA)
Shelter for Sophie (TBA)
Justice for Kinley (TBA)
Shelter for Promise (TBA)
Shelter for Koren (TBA)
Shelter for Penelope (TBA)

Beyond Reality Series

Outback Hearts
Flaming Hearts
Frozen Hearts

Writing as Annie George

Stepbrother Virgin (erotic novella)

Connect with Susan Online

Susan's Facebook Profile and Page:
www.facebook.com/authorsstoker
www.facebook.com/authorsusanstoker

Follow Susan on Twitter:
www.twitter.com/Susan_Stoker

Find Susan's Books on Goodreads:
www.goodreads.com/SusanStoker

Email: Susan@StokerAces.com

Website: www.StokerAces.com

To sign up for Susan's Newsletter go to:
http://bit.ly/SusanStokerNewsletter

Or text: STOKER to 24587 for text alerts on your mobile device

About the Author

New York Times, *USA Today*, and *Wall Street Journal* Bestselling Author Susan Stoker has a heart as big as the state of Texas, where she lives, but this all-American girl has also spent the last fourteen years living in Missouri, California, Colorado, and Indiana. She's married to a retired Army man who now gets to follow *her* around the country.

She debuted her first series in 2014 and quickly followed that up with the SEAL of Protection Series, which solidified her love of writing and creating stories readers can get lost in.

If you enjoyed this book, or any book, please consider leaving a review. It's appreciated by authors more than you'll know.

CPSIA information can be obtained
at www.ICGtesting.com
Printed in the USA
BVHW05s1040300718
523023BV00025B/937/P

9 780990 738862